The Prague Manuscript

Dr. James Paulding

Published by
Heritageheim Productions
9744 Elizabeth Street
Parker, CO 80134
Email: swpaulding@msn.com

German Specialist: Helga Paulding

Cover Photo: Prague, Czech Republic

Editor: Pam McKinnie, Concepts Unlimited

Design:
Concepts Unlimited
ConceptsUnlimitedInc.com
303-449-2907

ISBN: 978-0-615-31510-2   (pbk)

12   13   14   15   16   0 9 8 7 6 5 4 3 2

Printed in the USA

Dedicated to Karl Hausner.

With thanks to Hermine Hausner
for her continued support.

We also wish to thank Alfons Mader
for his help with various historical
aspects of this book.

*T*hey are coming closer, though still at the far end of the hall, a couple of helpers assisting a nurse as they move from door to door, bringing people out for lunch. Eventually everyone will move in small groups to the huge lift in the hallway and be transported down to the cafeteria. My turn will come in perhaps five or ten minutes. What language are the people here speaking? Czech? Polish? I really wish I knew. My second language is German.

I know I'm an American, but I have no idea where I am exactly. I have little memory of recent historical events, though I can remember the distant past most of the time, and also have vague recollections of friends and relatives. I know my name is Robert Westbrook, and I believe I was born in Denver, Colorado in 1978. Only a black and white photograph haunts my mind at present. The image returns again and again.

The structure where they are holding me is large, perhaps a home of some kind. There seem to be many elderly people here, which often makes me feel out of place because I am so much younger. Down in the cafeteria on the first floor is a long window running the length of the room. Outside this window I can see a lovely garden, but it tells me little except that I am not being held in a desert. Every other window in the home I can see is either painted over or boarded shut. There are no televisions, no newspapers,no computers. I have no knowledge of the outside world. Because of the language factor, though, I believe I am in eastern Europe.

While they have not attacked me physically here as yet, I am aware I am being drugged. I know they had given me at least one injection before I was brought here, but even now the drugs I receive are sometimes so powerful they knock me down completely and the helpers have to place me on my bed. Other times I am able to walk, though unsteadily. During these times I experience a kind of mild euphoria. Then I think it might not be too bad to stay in this place for awhile. Except for the dreams. Sometimes with the dreams, I wake up screaming!

One of the most horrible nightmares I had recently involved partisans beating civilians along some kind of road. Most of the partisans were wearing red arm bands, which made me think of communists at first, but I'm really not certain about this. Many of the people being beaten wore white armbands. As I think back on this scene, I am reminded of a place in Czechoslovakia known as the Sudetenland, where more than 3,000,000 Germans had been living, some for hundreds of years. These people were known as Sudeten Germans. They were driven out at the end of World War Two. In my dream I witnessed hundreds being savagely beaten. Some were young, many were elderly. It doesn't seem to matter. And yes, in this dream, too, I woke up screaming!

I am certain I have been here days, not hours. During this time no one has questioned me about anything. No one has mentioned my name. Considering the number of people working here, I am amazed I have heard no English, no German, only Czech or some Slavic language.

I awoke earlier this morning to the smell of paint. Perhaps because of the heavy amount of drugs I have been receiving, I had not noticed the smell before. I have tried repeatedly to open my window, but it is hopelessly stuck, probably because of the paint. I would like to open the window because I think then I might be able to see some mountains.

During the times I've been lucid, which is not much more than four or five hours a day, I have attempted to piece together some of the fragments of things which have been drifting through my mind. For example, while I know I was in Europe previously for some reason, I have no idea concerning the exact nature of my business here. There is also something about a bouquet of flowers, a Chicago connection, and the black and white photograph, which I suspect is many decades old. I remember there was a crowd of people in the photograph; perhaps they were watching a parade, or maybe a sporting event. At present, these are the only fragments of my more recent past I can recall, except, of course, the remembrances of friends and relatives which still remain with me.

Because I am being kept in this home against my will, I can only think either I have committed some terrible crime, or I have in my possession something important somebody wants. If either of the things is true, however, why has no one been talking to me? The nurses and helpers working here are professional in their manner and seem kind, but they appear to have no interest in me as an individual. I can honestly say no one seems to be watching me.

I believe at one time I was teaching at a university in Denver, but I cannot remember when I was first hired, or even whether I am still employed. I think I am in the humanities, perhaps history, but I cannot verify this. If my hunch is correct and I am being held somewhere in eastern Europe, I have no idea how I got here or why I came. The reason I am almost certain I am involved with history is because I seem to have a vast knowledge of the history of the western world, though certainly not recent history, which the drugs seem to have mostly erased.

Most of the dreams or nightmares I have been having because of the drugs, I do not recall in detail in the morning. One thing I do know, however, is when I have been tossing and turning earlier, I awake dead tired. I suspect my mind is more active in the night than in the day. God only knows where I go in the night. Sometimes I fear going to sleep.

It must have been on one of these nights, though, I began remembering more about the black and white photograph. The crowd in the background has come more into focus. The faces of the men are stoically optimistic; the women seem enthralled. I have seen this same love-death expression on the faces of women in the throes of sexual climax. Yes, it is right out of Wagner, all right. No doubt about it.

They have come to take me and others down to the cafeteria for lunch. Because I am tired this morning I roll to the lift in my wheelchair. As usual most other people on the lift are senior citizens. It is the same in the cafeteria. I am the only younger person in sight.

The lunch I am having here is in buffet style, though some of the very old people are served at their table. The mix of people is a strange one. Some I observe could be as young as fifty. And so, I ask myself, why are they here? All are Caucasian; in fact, as far as appearances go, they could be a group of white Americans getting together for lunch. Because of the language, though, I remain convinced I am somewhere in the East.

I take a bite from a slice of dark bread and wash it down with a sip from my second cup of coffee. Always, always, I am contemplating, trying to remember. Although I have no evidence to support my present supposition, I am almost certain there is a girl who is lost somewhere in this city, a girl who had originally accompanied me here.

Rolling out of the cafeteria after lunch, I wheel myself to the big lift, which takes me up to my room on the third floor. Actually I feel somewhat stronger now and so I decide to park my wheelchair in the hall near my room and take a short, careful stroll. I say 'careful' because my legs remain weak from lack of exercise and I am definitely wobbly.

At the end of one of the long hallways is the customary boarded-up window. What is out there, I wonder. A street? Is there perhaps a van parked down there with two men inside operating sound equipment? In their case, that's what I would be doing. I would be listening to every word I say, especially words coming from me to them in the night. In my drugged-up state I could be saying all sorts of things. And the mike? Where? Maybe in my ceiling lamp, or some place in my bathroom. Who knows? Perhaps their equipment is so sophisticated it can pick up sound right through the walls or windows.

I turn now to head back to my room. Far down this hall I see a man and woman approaching, who could be in their early forties. To my knowledge, I have never seen them before. We exchange silent greetings, not far from where I turn right to pause in front of my room. And then something notable occurs. Standing there by my door, I glance back toward the couple again. The woman has turned to stare at me. She is actually walking backwards and continues this until her escort gives her a nudge. I open the door to my room and lie on my bed. Except for the nurses and helpers, these two people are by far the youngest I have seen here.

Glancing toward the painted-over window eight feet away, I consider my state of mind. Although the feeling is sometimes subtle, I have noticed in the days since I have been held captive here, I have developed a strange fascination with the history of the Second World War. Now here I have no problem with memory. This history I know cold! I could give lectures about that war.

I suppose this fascination sprang from my growing up among many German and Czech families and hearing the stories the immigrant grandparents related about the 1930s and 40s back in Europe. Yet it cannot be these memories alone which are pulling me back in time; it is something far more forceful and more sinister. Into an age I could never have experienced first hand, into a war I could only have read about, only have seen snippets of on 16 mm film, a part of me still rushes back toward that age, seemingly helpless to resist the motion.

And out of the mental haze and fear something is finally coming into clear focus. I now completely understand the black and white photograph. I believe it wasn't a still shot at all, but rather 16 mm film footage and was originally, of course, in motion. The car, an open Mercedes, probably built sometime in the 1930s, moves slowly along through the dense crowds in the small city of Eger, Czecho-Slovakia. The beautiful bouquet of flowers is being presented by young children, ten or eleven years old. They, too, are in ecstasy because their arms and shoulders are being patted and stroked by a man who, as everyone knows, truly loves children. It is also his countenance which is causing certain of the women in the screaming crowds to swoon. This man is none other than the powerful Chancellor of Germany who, within a few months, will send an army into this entire land, occupying it. The army will enter in diagonals, and scarcely a shot will be fired. As Churchill said at one time, I believe: 'it is the end of the beginning'.

Well, Hitler's Mercedes has jump-started my memory once again. I swear, if my captors don't soon begin getting some additional drugs into my system, I will start remembering everything.

I had grown up in an upper middle-class neighborhood in Lakewood, Colorado. For as long as I can remember my father had owned a Mercedes dealership, and so we had always been regarded by others as being rather well-off. Although I had attended a public grade school, my parents had placed me in a private high school later, where I learned a great deal about European history. I continue to find it strange I can remember certain things concerning personal relationships, but very little about recent historical events.

When I observe myself in the mirror, I look to be in my early thirties and this seems about right. I appear to be the same six-foot-one in height I have always been as an adult. My hair is brown, my eyes sort of amber. I consider myself to be average looking, though I've known women who were quite capable of kidding me along, for one reason or another, telling me I'm hand-some.

Being held captive here in the East causes me once again to recall aspects of the 1930s and 40s. Although the Second World War was fought decades before I was born, I continue to wonder if there could possibly be some strange connection between where I am right now and that distant past. While my recent memory seems to have nearly vanished, I certainly remember German troops entering the Sudetenland following the Munich Pact in 1938. This had left a truncated state known as, Czecho-Slovakia.

In March of 1939, however, Czecho-Slovakia became the Protectorate of Bohemia and Moravia, while Slovakia became somewhat more independent. It is at this time Hitler enters Prague. Now the consistently cheering crowds are gone. From the official Mercedes one would have seen, not only the open hand Nazi salute coming from many Germans, but also the clenched fist coming from most disgruntled Czechs. The German soldier driving the Mercedes knows the crowd is not consistently friendly. His mouth is firm and set, and he is gripping the steering wheel so hard his knuckles are white.

Hitler, of course, is not always in a car. Sometimes he is seen walking on a street with one or more German officers. He is also seen just outside the great Prague castle, discussing something or other with a high-ranking Nazi official. (Was it Himmler? I can't remember.) One sees him standing at a window of the castle, high up, smiling and addressing the crowd below. Few Czechs, I believe, would have been in that audience. It was most certainly at about this time Bohemia and Moravia became the aforementioned German Protectorate. This couldn't have pleased the Czechs much either.

One has heard so many accounts about what actually happened during those days. It is said by some he was content during this time, even gleeful. What is he thinking as he stands at that high window looking down? That he has won?

Had he by then given up smoking? Did he ever give it up? It is said by many he almost never ate meat or drank alcohol. Can this be true? Others say it was true, but that he made an exception at this particular time. It was, after all, his springtime. A very human image to be sure—Adolf Hitler, sitting at the table there in the Prague castle, his feet perhaps resting on another chair, just relaxing. Surely the world is good now. No wonder he is smiling.

I take the time now to pinch myself on my upper arm. Not everyone at that moment in time is lounging around in a Czech castle. Tens of thousands of refugees have been on the move since 1938, Czechs leaving the border areas, German democrats, hating the Nazis, heading for Prague, or any other place they could find to lay their heads. Many of the social democrats were actually imprisoned.

And the Jews? Good Lord, who can help them now? Within a few months Hitler will invade Poland. And these refugees from the former Czechoslovakia? Well, although Germany would not take them, other nations did what they could to help. Even faraway America took five thousand people. And the synagogues were already burning like match sticks. It is the end of the beginning, all right.

One thing I feel in my heart. Knowing what I know now, had I been a professor or teacher at that art school in Vienna when he tried to enroll, I would have put my right arm around his shoulders and praised his work as high as the Grossglockner! Of course, he was interested in painting much earlier and I would have known it. I would have gazed seriously at his landscape paintings (some really not so terrible). I would have become his best friend, and we would have drunk strong coffee or beer together every afternoon after classes and discussed the world of art through the ages. Hell, considering what happened later, I would have been willing to spend the entire night discussing any subject he liked!

Excessive? Not so! Not so! Not so! Anything except invading Poland!

Whenever I lie here on my little bed getting depressed, which often happens when I think of Hitler, I fight it off, smile broadly, and remember a certain key. For if the missing girl, who I believe accompanied me to this ancient city, has followed my instructions, by now there is a key somewhere, most probably around her neck, or in one of her shoes. And I am becoming more and more convinced the reason I am being kept here in this home has something to do with the old Historic Provinces: Bohemia and Moravia, the epicenter of which is Prague. My thoughts are not drawn toward France, Italy, Russia, or Spain; my thoughts are centered on what was western Czechoslovakia. I am starting to believe something horrendous must have happened here years ago, and this girl, whose name I cannot quite remember, discovered what this was.

I am sick of staring at that painted-over window which seems to loom down at me from eight feet away. Sometimes I think I should get out of this bed, throw myself into my wheelchair again, and just race around the various halls, terrorizing the old folks. That might be fun. Instead, I turn my face to the wall and try and relax a little, try and work things out in my mind. I am not a composer, nor am I a painter or a scientist, so the leaders of this home must be concerned about something they think I have written.

But what? And where is it? And why is no one trying to find it? And does the girl really have a key somewhere? And what could be secured inside that locked entity? Surely nothing I have written. I vaguely remember, during the past five years my entire published work has been a small documentary film, which had sold a few DVDs in central Europe, and my Ph.D. dissertation dealing, I think, with the Austro-Hungarian Monarchy, which had sold not one copy. In fact, I doubt anybody in this entire land, except for perhaps a couple of professors, has ever heard of my thesis. Have I possibly completed another manuscript, the memory of which has been washed from my consciousness by their damned drugs? Possible, I suppose, but frankly I doubt it.

I continue staring at the wall, three feet away. Why are they holding me here? What is it they fear? I ball up my fists in frustration. Is someone in this city so afraid they are willing to commit criminal acts to keep me out of circulation, me, an American professor, who has no idea what he has done to terrorize them? I close my eyes, overwhelmed by a feeling of helplessness.

Pounding at the door! What the hell! Good Lord, I've fallen asleep without realizing it! The door opens and they are upon me, two young helpers holding me down, while an older man, perhaps about 45, gives me the needle. None of the three seem comfortable with their work, probably because they know damned well they are breaking somebody's law. The curious woman stands in the doorway viewing the scene with approval. I realize now she had been concerned to see me walking along the hall earlier, and figured they ought to give me the needle again to keep me helpless. Enjoy the moment, lady, I think. I'll get back at you sooner or later.

The two helpers have wrestled me into my wheelchair again and my God, my God, a nurse has grabbed onto the wheelchair and is pushing me so fast it makes me dizzy! It's all so crazy. The doctor who had given me the shots a couple of minutes ago did not in any way seem mean or oppressive to me, although his helpers were holding me down with all their strength. He just appeared to be doing his job in a professional manner, though why in hell he's working for the vicious woman who seems to be in charge of this home is more than I can fathom!

The nurse speeds us past two elderly women who are sitting in the hallway babbling to each other; then we race on to a small enclave where a lovely golden-haired lady is sitting before a boarded-up window. My Lord, it is Ruth Wedemeyer, a woman I met in Munich some time ago. Can she be a prisoner here too? I believe Ruth had been interested in some research I had been conducting, the subject of which I no longer remember. I thought she told me she had a position in the Catholic Church hierarchy, and was about to be transferred to Vienna. Or was it Berlin? She turns and meets my eyes. I am instantly aware that something has changed.

"You're not going to believe this, Robert, but I've joined an order. They tell me I'm to remain in flux. I guess you could say, I'm about to run away and live with Jesus." She is smiling at me now, perhaps trying to lessen the blow. She knows I'm in love with her.

Well, I think, if this is really true and you've joined an order, there will be a certain number of men who will find it difficult to understand. They'll consider it a waste. Some who know you well may become angry, especially those who had hoped for a relationship. I think I am about to tell Ruth this when suddenly I see she is gone. Vanished! My nurse wheels me around and we begin moving down the hallway in the direction of the big lift. I know exactly what is going on. I must have slept two hours or more, and it is now time for coffee and cake and afternoon activities. This is available for senior citizens every afternoon about this same time. In the lift I am aware my head is lolling around strangely and I am having trouble focusing. Those shots are really starting to hit home! I am not certain I can hold a fork for the cake, let alone a cup filled with coffee. Some helper may have to hand-feed me today.

The cake here is always small; the coffee usually cold, though in big cups. I think the cups are large. Today I can only see one clearly when it gets close to my mouth. Then the cupbearer taps my lips with the cup. Time to open up. I do so and nearly strangle while trying to drink. The cupbearer beats me on my back to save me and his efforts succeed. My vision is severely limited but I believe I noticed three or four ancient crones sitting at a nearby table, clapping heartily while I have been suffering.

Although I am squinting as best I can, I am only aware of vague forms around the room, many people playing cards, some gathering at the piano, no doubt to give the usual renditions of tunes, mostly in minor keys. I have been holding my cake in a shaky left hand, but now when I look for my fork, I see it has fallen from my right hand and is probably on the floor. Damn! A helper rushes forward, retrieves the fork, brushes it off on his trousers, and stuffs it into my right fist again. By God, I've got it this time! I'm strangling this fork like it was the neck of a chicken! I stab at my cake a little. Oh oh!

Cake is sliding to the left. Must come in more from the top. Stab. Stab. I'm unable to keep the small plate stable. Keeps leaning left. Slide, slide. I place my right eyeball four inches from the plate, hoping to spy my cake. Gone, naturally. So typical of this place. Someone on the sly has stolen it. I notice a few people are laughing at me.

One of the old gentlemen lurching by has struck my wheelchair, turning it about 20 degrees to the right. Even though I think I heard a sort of squish during the maneuver, I believe the motion was basically positive. Now my eyes can attempt to focus on a small area of a different scene. My problem, of course is the drugs. I am becoming more hallucinatory with every passing second.

I see two women at a chessboard quite near the far window, the window from which one can see the beautiful garden outside. I roll up to where they are sitting. White has moved pawn, E-5; black has moved pawn, E-4. White has a knight out front, part of a common plan. The two women's heads are resting on the table. They are either asleep or dead. I smile slyly at the knight.

"Go, horsey, go! Ride on! You practically have a clear field!" My own drugged-up head is nodding downward toward the table when I see, only vaguely, Ruth's hand reaching for the white knight. She picks it up and puts it into the pocket of her blouse. It is then I pass out.

When I awake much later I am in bed in my small prison room again. I am certain a couple of helpers have delivered me back here. The white knight is sitting upright on my bedside table. Viewing the chess piece, I naturally think of Ruth again. I am trying to persuade myself she is somewhere in this city trying to locate me. But the last I knew, she had taken a new position in Berlin, at least I think it was Berlin. I seem to recall we had some kind of argument about this decision.

I pick up the white knight now and examine it carefully. Could it possibly be a symbol of sorts? Could Ruth be suggesting that perhaps I am her white knight in real life? A bit simplistic, of course. Childish, in fact. Because by now my mind is clear enough to know Ruth was never present in this damned home. I was out of my head when I imagined her being here in the first place.

The two of us had met in Munich on a cool, sunshiny day last December. I was strolling back toward my rented Audi after visiting the Nymphenburg Palace. When I saw Ruth was alone and walking just ahead of me, I caught up with her, introduced myself, and invited her for coffee at a nearby cafe. Although this memory is still somewhat vague for me now, because of the drugs naturally, I actually believe I fell in love with her that same afternoon. It was a situation where two people meet and simply didn't want to give each other up. Afterward, we visited a large Christmas market where we enjoyed the music, the lights, and cups of steaming Gluehwein in the crisp Munich air. Later we had dinner in a downtown restaurant where she described her work with a children's organization, which was under the auspices of the Catholic Church.

Although Ruth is employed by the church, she was highly critical of certain of the excesses documented in history, mentioning the Spanish Inquisition and the killing of the Czech religious reformer, Jan Hus, among other things. I now remember sitting there watching her, her classical beauty occasionally unnerving me, keeping me a little off balance. Even five months later, thinking back, I don't believe I was ever before in the presence of such a beautiful woman.

Also during this dinner Ruth asked me about any research I had conducted recently. I believe I mentioned a documentary film I had completed five years ago, and said it dealt with a clash of cultures in eastern Europe in the aftermath of World War Two. Although she seemed fascinated by the subject matter, she warned me of possible dangers involved. I told her I thought the documentary had already been selling in Germany and Austria, and so it might be a little late to begin worrying. She told me then she was not thinking about Germany or Austria.

We wander the streets of downtown Munich until well after midnight, taking an hour or so out to visit a small bar and grill, where we have a few drinks and dance for awhile. By then we learned we are approximately the same kind of people, basically rather conservative, but with enough of a sense of adventure to keep boredom at bay. She refuses to accompany me back to my hotel, opting instead to meet me tomorrow morning after breakfast. We will leave for Salzburg, Austria shortly after ten o'clock.

Salzburg means Mozart and, even in the dawn of the 21st century, remnants of *The Sound of Music*. We stroll slowly up to the castle where we enjoy the view; then it's down to the city center again, where we window-shop for a couple of hours. We buy two Mozart Kugeln, a rich chocolate delicacy that almost everyone enjoys. As we walk along, nibbling at these delights, Ruth reminds me that Mozart himself never had the opportunity to partake of this small chocolate bullet, as they did not yet exist in his day.

We suddenly realize we have skipped lunch and so we find a nice restaurant and enjoy an early dinner. While we are having our salads, I believe Ruth again broached the subject of my documentary, warning me quietly it only takes about one-half of one percent of the population of any society to wreck havoc on a large scale. I seem to remember smiling and nodding my head.

"So, the truth does not make one free?" I ask.

She meets my eyes. "I'm sorry to be so negative, but sometimes the truth can make you dead!"

On the way back to Munich on the autobahn that evening we encounter a lot of traffic and, when I am not shifting gears, Ruth holds my right hand tight. I think she is telling me she trusts me now. It was on that return trip she told me about her parents, who had been killed in an automobile accident on the Brenner Pass while returning from Italy, leaving her, an only child, with a home and quite a lot of disposable income. Although Ruth is German, she had spent most of her young life in the Czech Republic. Her mother and father had moved to Prague from Germany before Ruth was born, because of business considerations. Her father had hired scores of Czech workers and so he and his wife were more than welcome in the Czech Lands. Following the deaths of her parents, she sold the family home near Prague and purchased a large apartment in Munich.

Ruth had attended a university in Germany because she can barely speak a word of Czech. She had earlier attended an international school in Prague, where she learned nearly perfect English. At the university in Munich she majored in religion and social science. I remember now what she said about some country other than Germany or Austria. Surely she had been referring to the Czech Republic. It is only now her remarks become clear to me.

Later that evening in my hotel room when we begin making love, she cries out and I realize she is a virgin. I become more gentle then and give her many soft kisses. By the time we finally fall asleep, I realize losing this girl would already constitute a tragedy for me. In the space of less than two days I have invested a great deal of my emotional well-being in this relationship.

During the following days we have a marvelous time: an afternoon in Garmisch, two nights in Friedrichshafen on Lake Constance and, since Ruth was interested in the murder of Jan Hus, we also visit the city of Constance on the other side of the lake where the actual burning of the outspoken Czech leader occurred.

The money for these wonderful escapades is coming from my parents, who evidently have sufficient funds to lavish on their only son. While I believe I have recently risen to the rank of associate professor, this just makes me part of the shrinking American middle class. On my own, I would not have had enough money to vacation in Europe. Only my father, with his Mercedes dealership, makes this possible.

I had called ahead for opera tickets for a production of *Die Fledermaus* on New Year's Eve in Vienna, as well as a night at the Sacher Hotel afterwards. We actually check into our room shortly after twelve o'clock and then head down to a cafeteria where we order two pieces of Sacher cake with whipped cream. My position is: if the people here can't make Sacher Torte, no one in the world can. We have ordered plenty of coffee and it is while we are sipping our second cup that Ruth mentions certain plans she has for the coming spring.

"Bob, I don't want to appear forward, but in late April I will have an additional two weeks of vacation. I would like to come and visit you in Colorado."

"Lord, Ruth, that's just great! We'll spend a few days in the mountains." We are both smiling as we consider this plan. But I'm also thinking about something else near term. "Ruth, perhaps we could go up to our room now. Get a little rest in anticipation of tonight's big performance." I am trying not to leer.

She laughs. "Bob, you're a madman! You should spend more time studying the philosophy of the Greeks." She hesitates and continues to watch me. "'Nothing in Excess'. I know you've heard that little gem before." She laughs again. "But I do agree with you about going upstairs. As a matter of fact, I believe an afternoon nap is entirely appropriate."

Die Fledermaus was a huge hit, and during intermission when we look outside, we see it is snowing. Vienna, New Year's Eve, 'The Bat', and falling snow. I don't think it ever gets any better than this!

The painted-over window draws my eyes toward it as usual. I have to get out of this room for awhile! I decide on another short walk, heading in the same direction I had taken when I met the man and woman hours earlier. This time, however, I turn left when I reach the end of the hall. All three windows I pass are either painted-over or boarded shut.

At the far end of this hall is a large chair. I am astonished to find it is rather comfortable. I decide to stay here for a few moments. I find myself considering a timeline now, something which could turn out to be important to my present situation.

After completing my Ph.D. in the fall, I had flown to central Europe, as usual at my parents' expense, to relax for a few weeks. The time stretching to early January is fairly clear in my mind, mainly I believe because I had met Ruth then, and she had dominated my thoughts. After all, I am still confident I am going to marry this girl.

I left Ruth soon after our visit to Vienna during New Years, this in order to return to my university in Denver for the spring semester. My memory is obviously improving. 24 hours ago I would have had no idea whether I was still employed in the state of Colorado. I'm also beginning to think the doctor, who had given me the needle earlier, had purposely cut back on the dosage. I'm recovering faster than usual this time.

An important question with which I need to come to grips is: why did I return to Europe again recently? I remember quite clearly Ruth was making plans to visit me in Denver this spring. What had kept her from making the trip? Although it might seem natural for me to worry, I really do not believe something terrible has happened to Ruth. Due to the fact I distinctly remember her discussing a new job, I am almost positive she is now in Berlin. Obviously, there are still problems with my memory regarding the weeks between the first part of January and the beginning of May. I need to continue to think about these few months.

I glance down the long hallway from where I still sit comfortably in my large chair. I squint a little, trying hard to remember things. I envision three Mercedes automobiles. They float through my mind in sequence. I picture my father standing by one of his larger white models, looking inside at a customer seated behind the wheel. Perhaps they are discussing a purchase.

Another Mercedes, this time an open one. It is moving slowly along in a place called the Sudetenland in Czecho-Slovakia. Adolf Hitler often stands, waving to the worshipping crowds, most of whom have their arms extended in a Nazi salute. Although most of these citizens carry Czech ID papers, in terms of culture and language, they are German.

The third Mercedes is a lighter colored one, which I had rented in Bavaria a few days ago, just before being abducted. A girl is seated on my right. She is the *second girl*, someone I had met a scant four months earlier. She stares straight ahead into the eastern sky. We leave Germany, crossing into the Bohemian Forest, moving relentlessly toward the ancient, bloody city of Prague. She will enter this city like a thief in the night, leaving me alone with a target on my back. We will separate with scarcely a word of goodbye, right after I order her to get a key and hide the manuscript.

At the moment I still cannot remember her name, though I am positive the name is lurking somewhere in my mind. She had once become angry with me about the 'name problem'. But others knew her name and they had let me know about it in no uncertain terms. She had also accused me of not liking her, but that wasn't quite fair because I had hardly known her at the time. When I think of her I become uneasy because I know something is wrong with her emotionally. She sometimes takes chances which are over the line, and encourages others to do the same. Just a few weeks ago she suggested I lie, in order to obtain money. A lot of money! Money, which for her would have meant nothing! But she loved the excitement of my gambling with the facts.

A name like the changing of the seasons.

The name should already have come to me because of her father, the western senator, whose family had made their vast fortune in Montana, Wyoming, and Colorado mining, whose wife had divorced the senator early on because of his scandalous ways, changing mistresses as often as he changed the oil in his sports cars, the lone daughter more or less abandoned, running loose on the streets of Denver, her jeans stuffed with fifty-dollar bills, her mind filled with God knows what.

But now, I think back to the beginning of this story.

It is January, four months before we finally separated on that late spring afternoon in Prague. Now it is winter and, here in Denver, Colorado, it is snowing. She is sitting quietly in a chair outside my office on the first day of the new semester. When she notices me walking slowly toward her she stands, ready to join me for her first conference.

"I'm the girl who called," she tells me. "Everly Somerset. And you are Dr. Westbrook."

I nod and usher her inside my small office. My first impression is she is pretty, but I soon realize she is just as beautiful as Ruth in her own way, though her beauty is tastefully understated. Today she is dressed conservatively, cream-colored slacks and a yellow blouse, which blend perfectly with her light brown hair. She is carrying a brown coat over her arm, and has some papers in her right hand. Although I have never seen this girl in my life, I already smell trouble. I'm convinced some crafty individual has sent her to me.

"How is it you decided to approach me in particular?" I ask her. We are now seated on opposite sides of my large desk. I notice she has very bright eyes, green as in a raging sea. I watch as she lays her papers on my desk.

"I read your dissertation dealing with the Austro-Hungarian Monarchy. Quite good, really. You write better than most professors around this campus. Few people care about writing these days. Short little sentences, accompanied by lots of numbers and boring facts. I also know your documentary film, describing the murders that occurred at the end of World War Two. I viewed it five or six times." She hesitates for a second or two. "Of course, you are rather young, but that's probably okay. At least you do things."

So, she's a smart ass, I am thinking. Still, I give her a half smile. "I might be able to help you locate a more mature advisor," I say. "I could put you in touch with a few learned professors who are nearing 80. I can only guess they are highly intelligent men who live only for their students. After all, what other reason might they have for hanging around the campus, taking up space?" Although I have tried to keep the conversation on a lighter vein, I notice she has not smiled once.

"I'm interested in the Sudetenland," she says abruptly. "My grandfather on my mother's side was murdered there in 1945. He was a German soldier."

"SS? Those most fearsome of all German fighters?"

"No, a common soldier. 18 years old. He married my grandmother in March of that year. She was 16. She was raped by partisans later in the spring, actually during the 'Bruenn Death March'."

I frown and shake my head, letting her know I am sorry. "And so, you wish to concentrate on the aftermath of the big war in what is now the Czech Republic."

"As well as the history of the three main provinces: Bohemia, Moravia, and that strip of Silesia on the Czech side."

"Few students would attempt to cover such an overwhelming topic in an M.A. thesis. Your research alone could total hundreds of pages."

"Are you interested in helping me, or not? We need to talk more about this."

"I am willing to discuss your ideas. That's what I'm here for." I pause for a moment. "It's quite a coincidence. My German girl friend grew up near Prague."

"I want to meet her." No hesitation.

"Well, you'll probably get your chance. She's planning to visit me here in Colorado this coming spring."

"How wonderful!" She stands and turns toward the door.

"Ms. Somerset?" She pauses. "At what age did you enroll in our university?"

"17. That was five years ago. Have you never examined my file?"

"No, but I soon will."

"A good idea," she says, and leaves my office, disappearing into the hall.

That afternoon I learn more about her. According to the letters in her file, Everly Somerset is a workaholic who operates at the genius level. She seems to have reformed since her days roaming the streets of Denver.

Sitting here in my comfortable chair in my prison home, staring down the long hallway, recalling my feisty graduate student, I suddenly remember the name of my documentary film. It is called *Brothers at War*, and it sold quite well in central Europe. I also notice I am hungry, no doubt because I somehow lost my cake earlier in the afternoon.

I stand and walk back toward my room. I definitely feel stronger now. Though I may fail, I intend to try and break out of this place later tonight. There may never be another chance. I remember the doctor who had given me the injection, but who had purposely cut back on the dosage. Thank you, Doctor. I consider you to be a moral person. You've at least given me the possibility of escaping sometime during the next three or four hours.

It is already late afternoon. I will be lucky if I can still get some food in the cafeteria. I will take the wheelchair down, even though this is unnecessary. But the last thing I need is to appear a strong young male, completely in charge of his facilities. That would be a certain invitation for another injection.

In the cafeteria I find only ten or twelve people. I am happy to see there is still food at least. As usual, it is strange to look around at the others having dinner, knowing there is no way I can converse with them. I carefully listen to the various conversations and hear only Czech or some other Slavic language. I would bet $1,000 it is Czech. As usual, I am the only younger person in evidence, and when I glance at the others they usually avert their eyes, in fear, or perhaps embarrassment. How I would love to have a German or English newspaper so I could catch up on world and American news.

When I roll the wheelchair over for more coffee I see them again through the open doorway, the middle-aged couple. They are just leaving a room down the hall. This time they are accompanied by two younger men who are wearing some kind of uniform. The four are heading this way, probably hoping for a late cup of coffee. Entering the cafeteria, they get their coffee and take a table about 20 feet away from me. The woman stares at me for a few seconds and then turns away. I imagine she is confident I am so full of drugs I am not going anywhere except back to my room. I have a feeling the woman and her three companions may be discussing my future. A dismal thought.

When I finally leave the cafeteria, I move the wheelchair slowly, as though the task is almost beyond me. I roll toward the large lift, sometimes pausing as though needing to gather more strength before continuing. I am not certain the four strangers are watching me, and I really don't care. This is all a charade anyway, because I feel stronger now than I have in days.

Back in my little room on the third floor I lie on my bed again, knowing I will need to wait at least a couple of hours until I make my move. I wish I could latch onto a weapon or two, but I have no idea where to get them. I was always rather good with a pistol or revolver. I had noticed the two soldiers in the cafeteria were armed. My mind is even clearer now, though I realize I still need to think about those months between January and May. I need to fully comprehend how I happened to end up a prisoner in this place. Surely Everly had nothing to do with it. Although I know she has her personal obsessions, I'm convinced she would never wish me harm.

I think back now to the first time the university administration interfered with me regarding Everly. It was the same afternoon I first read her file. The call was from the university's vice president, Dr. Melvin O'Roark. At first the conversation remained pleasant, though I did think I detected tension in his voice. In the end, however, his message was harshly simple: "Senator Somerset is a powerful man, who is by far the largest contributor to our university in the entire history of the school, and his young daughter is presently in your care. Everyone hopes her thesis dealing with past upheavals in what is now the Czech Republic will be a success." He had replaced his receiver before I had a chance to reply to what amounted to a veiled threat.

That same day I was able to research the story of Ms. Somerset's grandfather at the end of the Second World War. From her file I learned her grandfather's name was Franz Leopold Hauptmann and that he had indeed been a young soldier. But, when I later pulled up additional information from German and Czech sources, the two reports diverged. The Germans say only that

Private Hauptmann served in the German army and had been killed in early May, 1945 as the war was ending. The Czechs reported he had been a member of the much feared SS, that he had killed three Czech civilians in early April of that year, and was later put to death because of these criminal acts.

And so it goes. In war, most governments find it expedient to lie like common crooks! I suppose Ms. Somerset can take her choice as to what to believe. My hunch is she'll stand by the German report. She'll figure the Czechs killed plenty of their own German people after the war, whether they were SS, or not.

Three days later she called for another appointment. When she came in shortly after nine o'clock the following morning, she dumped 70 or so additional pages on my desk. When I flip through some of them I see familiar names: Pilsen, Aussig, Landskron, Bruenn, scores of others, usually the German spelling instead of the Czech. I have promised myself I will remain pleasant, but I am bothered by something.

"Ms. Somerset, I surely hope you are not planning to copy the script of my documentary film of five years ago, and now turn it in as your M.A. thesis."

She meets my eyes. "Dr. Westbrook, please examine these pages carefully. You will find the writing exemplary and my approach captivating."

My God, I think, what a conceited little ball buster! But she rolls right over me.

"Now here is the plan of action for this semester. After examining many theses here in our library, I realize I will need to pare my own work considerably."

"Which means?"

"Let me explain. My completed manuscript will be in excess of 700 pages. But, for the thesis, I suggest cutting it to 160. Are you following?"

"Why not limit your subject so 160 pages cover the entire topic? Choose only certain sections of the country and deal with whatever happened there. And frankly, your dream of completing a manuscript of 700 pages, well, that's a lot of keyboard work." I gaze at her. "Have you really considered this plan carefully?"

"You don't understand. It is the large book that is important to me. I intend to uncover every atrocity that ever occurred in that Slavic land!"

"Where are you getting your facts?"

"Don't worry. I'll probably tell you one day."

"I'd like you to tell me about the facts now, Ms. Somerset. Otherwise, you can look for another advisor."

"You'll never be able to get rid of me. The administration has decided you're the one. Why, I don't know." She smiles at me. "They want you to look after me."

"You're 22, and filthy rich! You don't need me or anybody else."

"Maybe not, but they're making you responsible. But please, Dr. Westbrook, don't become overly concerned. I'll soon explain the source of my facts." She takes a deep breath. "And you should know something else. The main reason I am here today is that my father and certain members of this administration continue to pressure me into earning an advanced degree. If I had my way, I would just hire you or some other professor privately to help me complete my big manuscript. I don't care about the degree."

"But have you no interest in using your M.A. later as a teacher, or a writer perhaps?"

"Probably not. I'm concentrating more on the short run. You surely know by now I don't need a job." She laughs.

I nod. "But this morning you've worried me just a little. You seem somewhat obsessed with your manuscript. I guess I don't understand what you intend to do with it."

Seconds pass. I notice there is a faint smile on her face. "I want to use it to get even," she says finally.

"Get even?" I stare at her.

"Yes. Get even. I intend to cause some disruption in certain areas of central Europe." She then points down to the pages she has already given me. "You will find an index covering these," she adds.

"Admirable."

"And, Dr. Westbrook, do you even know my first name? It seems somewhat stiff to continue referring to me as Ms. Somerset."

Oh boy, now she has me! I really have forgotten her first name!

"I believe I should continue addressing you as Dr. Westbrook, but you should begin addressing me as Everly. After all, I am only a lowly student."

Sure you are, I think, and I'm starting to wonder just how much money you really do have. But I need to keep myself under control. "Of course, I must remember your first name," I say quietly. "And in the future, I promise I won't forget it."

She is watching me carefully. "I have a feeling you don't like me much."

"Ms. Somerset, ah, Everly, I really don't know you that well yet. But I have a feeling you are eventually going to impress the hell out of me!"

She stands and turns toward the hall. "I'll call you," she says evenly.

When Everly has gone I think of Ruth again. Since the time I left Munich after my Christmas break, Ruth and I have kept in constant touch by phone and e-mail. I usually take a late lunch about two o'clock and drive to my small house near the university and call her. By then it is ten o'clock at night in Germany. A couple of days ago I mentioned Everly, saying I had a graduate student who is smarter than I am.

"Is she pretty?" Ruth asked immediately, laughing a little.

"Sort of. She scarcely stays around long enough for me to notice. She wishes me good morning and then flops another bunch of papers on my desk. She wants to meet you when you're here in the spring."

"That's fine." She hesitates for a couple of seconds. "I miss you, Bob. Those days we were together during Christmas vacation were the best days of my life. Vienna and the snow."

"They were magical, all right. But, Ruth, you know in Europe we spent a great deal of time traveling around, having one marvelous experience after another. When you're here in Colorado, though, we need to discuss a few serious matters."

"Sounds interesting. Sure you don't want to discuss them right now?"

"No." I laugh. "In the springtime. In the Rockies. It will be more romantic."

"Okay, then. Goodnight, Bob." I can hear her kisses coming all the way from Munich.

This was, of course, all in the past. Here in my prison home it is already springtime. The crazies nabbed me the same evening Everly and I had separated here in Prague. She is now wandering around alone in this city, and Ruth is probably already in Berlin.

Although I no longer have a watch, I believe I still need to wait at least another hour before attempting my escape. I want it to be completely dark. My concern is if I don't make it out of here tonight, the crazy woman in charge of this place may order additional drugs be given me in the morning.

As I lie here on my bed, staring at my painted-over window, my thoughts turn to Everly again. I remember I did not hear from her again until the beginning of the following week. In the meantime, I found a major historical error in her treatment of the Thirty Years War. I was led to this mistake by way of her index, which had included the name, Wallenstein. I turned back to the interior page, the number of which had been listed after the name, and find she evidently believes the armies of the Holy Roman Empire had been led by Albrecht von Wallenstein against the Bohemians in the major battle of White Mountain near Prague on November 8, 1620. The actual general in charge was Johannes Tilly, imperialist general in the Thirty Years War. It is an indisputable fact that it was Tilly's forces that broke through the Protestant lines that day, destroying the dreams of the Bohemians, who had hoped they might obtain independence from the Austrian Hapsburgs with a victory. Although Wallenstein won many battles for the Catholic cause in that war, he just didn't happen to be at White Mountain on that eighth of November. I'm surprised Everly didn't know this.

While back at the University I had not spent much time examining this thesis. Frankly, the work depresses me. Not only is it so well written it makes me feel somewhat inferior, it is also exciting in a kind of shocking way, as Everly approaches the aftermath of the Second World War from the German perspective, creating an empathy for the Sudeten Germans which I am certain would disturb many Czechs. But this young woman does not really need my help with her thesis. She doesn't need help from anyone.

The title of her work is, *The Prague Manuscript: Czech crimes against German and Hungarian Civilians, 1945-46.* When I glance at the work, however, I see she had also dealt extensively with the entire history of what had been Czechoslovakia. Thinking back, I would never have guessed how her words would change my life, and how much danger they would expose me to in just a few short months.

And so, why isn't Everly Somerset being held here in this home? I smile and shake my head. The answer probably is that no one knows about her outside of Denver, Colorado. The national print media was responsible for this, having dropped her name from their articles, in effect, making me the sole author of the large manuscript.

The afternoon before my next meeting with Everly, I received a call from the editor of our university newspaper, asking for permission to join us tomorrow morning. He wants to bring his camera along and get some shots of Everly and myself together. He would also like an interview, focusing on her thesis, as well as some larger manuscript which came to his attention. He has, of course, heard about the murders but, from his attitude, I think he believes they occurred just last week. We meet at nine o'clock.

The young man finishes his photography in about ten minutes and then the three of us huddle around my desk, while Everly and I talk about her thesis. She is quite honest in admitting she is writing the large manuscript from the German point of view, which she insists has not been adequately covered to date. (I'm actually not certain about this, but I don't interrupt.) She also relates the story of her soldier grandfather and his death at the end of the war, being careful not to mention the fearsome SS.

I take over then, pointing out the high quality of Everly's writing and suggesting the thesis also makes for an interesting read, not surprising considering the subject matter. When the young editor asks Everly how many innocent Germans were killed in 1945-46, she immediately replies: "Many thousands!" For me, this seems an honest answer, especially when I recall older Germans in places like Nuremberg and Augsburg telling me more than 130,000 Germans were killed at that time. Everly's vague answer seems to be more on point, because present-day citizens of Germany and the Czech

Republic still hold wildly differing views about what really happened back then. But in her writing, I'm certain Everly is taking the German side.

As we approach what I am assuming must be the end of the interview, Everly shocks me by bringing up my documentary film, *Brothers at War*. When the editor realizes that my film also deals with German and Czech citizens after the big war, he pounces! He questions me thoroughly about my premise, and asks both of us to explain the connection between my older work and Everly's thesis. After a couple of minutes I raise my hand and call a halt to the questions. I remind the young man that my film was created five years ago, and we were supposed to be discussing Ms. Somerset's thesis, which is much more detailed than my small DVD, which is a scant 30 minutes in length. But then Everly prolongs the conversation by telling the editor that *Brothers at War* had sold hugely in both Germany and Austria and, by the way, might he perhaps wish to view the film? Not waiting for a reply, she pulls a white carrying case from her purse and hands it to him.

My first thought is she is hoping the editor will write a negative article, suggesting her thesis topic be banned due to its nearly identical subject matter as her advisor's small film. This would probably free her from having to write a thesis at all! At the moment, I can think of no other reason for her actions. None at all. I had not yet realized that Everly Somerset had a much larger agenda in mind, an agenda which, when finally brought to light, would scare the hell out of me!

After the young editor left us, I gave her a hostile stare. "Well, I guess I am finally forced to believe you. You really don't give much of a damn about our M.A. program!"

"I told you, I don't like pressure. But whatever happens, I am going to hire you to help me with the large work." She is smiling now. "My 700 plus pages of horror. Don't worry, I've plenty of money to pay you. By law my father had to give me a settlement four years ago when I turned eighteen. Want to know what I'm worth?"

"No!" At that moment the phone rings. It is Vice President O'Roark again. He asks me how the interview went. I tell him we had gotten through it and had also posed for a few photographs. But when he asks if Everly is still here,

I lie and say I believe she has gone to the library. He hangs up. I turn back to my graduate student.

"You know, Everly, there is no reason for you to share personal information with me. Your private life is none of my business."

She hesitates, smiling again. "Wouldn't you like to know when I finally reformed and gave up running around loose on the streets? I'll bet you've heard about my past."

"I'm not interested. I guess I'm glad you reformed but again, this is none of my business. There is something, though. Wallenstein. He wasn't the general at White Mountain that day. It was Johannes Tilly who was in charge of the Catholic forces on the 8th of November, 1620."

"Are you certain? I guess I just assumed it was Wallenstein because of how much I had read about him, and because of his magnificent palace in Prague."

"Don't ever assume," I tell her. "It was just lucky I happened to spot the error." She doesn't bother thanking me.

She stands and turns toward the door. But she stops then and looks back at me. "Dr. Westbrook, I promise you Wallenstein will be the last mistake I ever make on your watch." She gives me a small wave and disappears into the hallway.

The article appeared three days later with an accompanying photograph depicting me as an overly serious academic type, and Everly as a beautiful girl, appearing even younger than her 22 years. The article itself is fine, although I would have preferred they spent less time discussing my documentary film. But at least they gave Everly's thesis good coverage at the beginning. My major concern is that she is presenting the history as though she assumes most scholars have already concluded the Czechs were guilty of committing more than 130,000 murders after the war. Everly never seems to question the possibility that some people, especially those in the Sudeten community, might have exaggerated the number of atrocities for decades. She is leaning so far toward the German side, I sometimes wonder if she isn't occasionally hearing voices in the night supporting her positions. I, however, am hearing no voices, and I worry no person in sight is speaking up for the

Czechs in this thesis. But, whatever the true numbers were, I'm well aware, for the Sudeten Germans, the mid 1940s had been a very bad time indeed.

The Sunday edition of the *Denver Mountain Guardian* garbled the story completely. In the first place, the only photograph is one of me, which I assume they obtained from the university. The article is headed, 'Denver Professor Assists Young Student in Solving Murders'. In the very first paragraph *Brothers at War* is discussed, mentioning how successful my documentary had been earlier in Germany and Austria.

Nowhere in the article is the Czech Republic mentioned; in fact, there is only a vague reference to murders committed somewhere in eastern Europe. Everly's name appeared one time when it was stated: "Everly Somerset, young daughter of Senator Charles Somerset, is working with Dr. Westbrook in attempting to shed light on certain atrocities taking place after the Second World War in Europe." I believe some readers might think Everly is a girl in high school.

Monday morning I received an additional call, this time from Dr. Harald Haverkamp, President of the University. Cutting right to the core, he asked me who in hell provided the Denver paper with such misleading information, and why am I advertising my own film instead of discussing Ms. Somerset's thesis, which should be my main concern. I naturally tell him I have not spoken with anyone at the newspaper, and I agree Everly Somerset's thesis should remain my highest priority. I do not remind him of the fact that I am also teaching three sections of European History, with each class overflowing with at least 80 students.

A week goes by. Everly has given me another batch of pages and we have agreed she should remain in the M.A. program, at least for the time being. But now my life is about to change. I received a long e-mail from someone in Lake Forest, Illinois and, later that same day, a phone call from, I believe, the same person. This individual sounds young on the phone, and has a strong German accent. From his e-mail I already know he wants me to fly to the Chicago area as soon as convenient. He now explains that a recent article in a Chicago newspaper has led him to believe we need to have a face-to-face conversation. He continues with scarcely a hesitation. If I really am Dr.

Robert Westbrook, the professor who created the documentary film, *Brothers at War*, and who is presently writing a weighty manuscript, listing the hundreds of atrocities that occurred in what is now the Czech Republic in 1945-46, then there must be a meeting. Preferably soon! He then tells me there could be a substantial amount of money available for my new project. He suggests he call me tomorrow at this same time for my answer. I agree to this and quickly wish him 'auf wiedersehen'.

But now, I return to the present. It is time for me to attempt an escape from this prison. I put on my light brown jacket, which I was wearing the night I was abducted, and simply walked down the stairs and out what I believe to be the main door of the home. It is the door near the beautiful garden I have so often admired. I have not a cent of money on me, nor any identification. The only plan I have is to flag down a taxi, give the name of the American Embassy and pretend I have money to pay the taxi driver for the trip.

But I do not get far. The two younger men I saw earlier wearing the strange uniforms stop me before I even reach the main street. Ordinarily I would have run for it, as I am just as young and basically just as fit as my captors, but because of what they put me through recently, I simply lack the strength for any kind of confrontation or footrace. The men do not yell, nor do they rough me up. Without saying a word, they simply put me back in the home. I nod to them, get into the big lift, take it up to the third floor, and walk to my room.

But I do not give up yet. 30 feet beyond my room to the left is another hallway which leads to a much smaller elevator. There is no room for a wheelchair here, but I'm not in a wheelchair any longer. I also know this lift, just like the much bigger one, descends down to the kitchen, which is one floor lower than the floor where the flower garden is outside, and the main door from which I tried to escape a few minutes ago.

I wait 20 minutes and then try my new plan. The small lift makes practically no sound, and the kitchen on the lowest floor is empty. I can't believe my luck! I am also in semidarkness, which helps. There must be an emergency door leading from the basement area outside. I find this door in less than a minute. The main writing is Slavic, but there are older, fainter letters as well. NOTAUSGANG, the German phrase reads "Emergency exit." The writing does not surprise me.

The question now is whether or not I'll hear bells and whistles when I crack this door a little. I can't think of anything to be gained by waiting. I push the door open. Total silence. Wonderful! Can escaping really be this easy? Although it is still night, of course, it is certainly not pitch dark. There is enough light for me to maneuver. There is a half-moon, and the street lights from this part of the city are helping as well.

And now, do I make a run for it, or creep stealthily along near the shrubbery? I decide to move slowly, keeping my body as low as possible. I have a good idea where I am in relation to the place the two men caught me before, which was several yards to the right of my present position. I am already perhaps 45 yards from the home itself when I run into a high fence. No problem, I think. All I need to do is move quietly along the fence to my left until I come to a large opening. This will be the opening trucks use to bring supplies into the home. I have often heard these vehicles moving in and out from my painted-over third floor window above.

I begin slowly moving to my left, treading as softly as I can. Within less than five minutes I can see the vague outline of the opening where the trucks enter during the day. Obviously there is a street there. The trucks have to come from someplace.

And now the great temptation is to run for it, run right down that street in front of me, run until there is no more strength left in me. And then perhaps fight for my freedom. But after some consideration I decide against this alternative. I must face reality. There are still so many drugs in my body, of one kind or another, my only hope is to proceed at a more leisurely pace.

It turns out neither of these plans matter anyway. Soldier number one steps out from his place in the shadows, holding a revolver. He then blows twice on a whistle. Soldier number two comes running up within seconds. He, too has a revolver, threatening me. I waggle the forefinger of my right hand at both of them, strongly hinting they should settle down.

Soldier number one is still poking his revolver toward me with his right hand, while his left hand points upward at the home to where he thinks my room might be.

"Put your guns away," I tell them both, not really knowing whether they can understand English. In German, I tell them I will go with them willingly. I don't know if they understand German either. They look at each other like they don't know what to do.

"The front door," I say, pointing in that direction. "The emergency exit will already be closed for the night." After a brief hesitation, the three of us walk at deliberate speed toward the main door. Their weapons are by now out of sight, just as I wanted them to be.

Soldier number one goes with me on the big lift to the third floor, and then down the hallway to my room. He pulls up a chair, planning, I think, to spend the night outside my door. I put both my hands together and place them against my right cheek, my head tilted slightly to the right, the universal sign of a baby sleeping. Then I point to his chair and laugh aloud. He is scowling at me. I enter my room and close the door. Good luck, soldier, I think. Get a good night's rest. And myself? Well, I really do sleep pretty much just like a baby.

In spite of the excitement of the previous night, I awake about seven o'clock. My major concern at the moment is that the gang with the long thin steel will soon be coming to visit me again, led of course by the sinister woman who seems to be in charge of this place. Because I have developed no plan of action as yet, I simply walk down the hall to the big lift, take it down to the cafeteria, and eat a normal breakfast there.

After breakfast I return to my room, strolling along at a normal pace. There is no sense pretending I am still under the influence of drugs. The report on me from last night will already be in. And so, I wait. With no weapon, I am at their mercy. Lying on my bed again, the window looms over me as usual. I try and stare it down. Thinking back, I realize it was my very next meeting with Everly which started me along the path that led directly to this prison home. Even now, I have trouble believing it.

The two of us met in a large student hangout, later on the same day I had received the E-mail and phone call from Lake Forest, Illinois. I remember we were eating cheeseburgers and drinking German beer in one of the establishment's back booths. She seemed not to care what I do.

"You want to follow this up? Go for it! It might even be advantageous. You can just keep the German guy's donation. As you know, I don't need it."

"I've told you I'm certain he believes I am the one writing the large manuscript."

"So? Put your name on it. It's okay by me."

I stare at her. "I'm not following. Before, you seemed preoccupied with your large work, yet now you claim it doesn't matter if I take credit for it. Strange."

"Why are you so worried? Look, either you accept this man's donation, or forget about the whole thing. But why shouldn't you accept the money? It sounds like they are practically begging you to take it." She grins at me. "I'll purchase two plane tickets to Chicago. I'm going with you."

"Why, for God's sake?"

"Easy. I have something else to do there. Need to meet someone special." She laughs. "Also, I believe there is an even chance you'll receive this donation in cash. I doubt you will ever learn this man's name. For all we know, he may be an old Nazi."

"You're welcome to your opinion, but the man I spoke to on the phone today sounded decidedly young."

"Okay. But you are meeting someone with a German accent in a mansion in Lake Forest. They are not inviting you out there to present you with some paltry check for five or six thousand dollars. I won't go with you to the meeting, of course. You can drop me off some place and then pick me up later. But I'm flying with you to Chicago. This is just the kind of excitement I thrive on!"

"Shouldn't I order the plane tickets?"

She is laughing now. "Haven't you ever wondered why the president and vice president of our university call you occasionally? Somebody mentions my name, the administrators turn pale and practically pee their pants. Dr. Westbrook, the inheritance my wayward father was forced by law to give me four years ago begins with the letter 'B'."

I shrug. "Okay then, get the tickets. When the German guy calls tomorrow I'll tell him I'm coming. I'll also cancel my classes for two days."

"Good idea, because I doubt we'll be returning to Denver by plane."

For a few seconds we are silent as we deal with our cheeseburgers. I watch her as she chews. Jesus, she is like a lioness who has just caught a small animal in the bush and is now devouring it. "We'll need to discuss how I'm to handle the Lake Forest meeting," I say finally.

"You'll obviously have to lie. No one will ever believe I wrote *The Prague Manuscript*."

Why the past tense? I wonder. Perhaps I didn't understand her. I watch as she wolfs down the last big bite of the cheeseburger. "When did you decide on your title?"

"When I was 17. The same year I first viewed your small film, the year I entered the university, which was right after I came in off the streets." She is laughing at me now. "I think it may be necessary for us to form an alliance. You may have to decide whether to stand with me, or the university administration."

"If we go to Lake Forest together, I guess we'll have to stand by each other."

"You sure?"

"Yes. You see, I dislike politicians generally, and I'm not overly fond of either the president or vice president of our university. Let me relate a dream I had once." I take another swig of beer and continue. "I stand on Pikes Peak on a perfectly clear day. I can see into Kansas. Every ten feet or so I see bodies hanging. Thousands of them. They are either politicians, or idiots who argue for political correctness."

She laughs again. "That's the exact kind of dream I have occasionally. Maybe we're the same kind of people." She drains the last fourth of her beer in two big gulps. "Let's get out of here. I have something to show you back in my oversized home. It may shock you. You sure we stand together?"

I glance down at my half finished beer and decide to leave it. "Let's go. I'll follow you in my car." I already know she drives a BMW convertible.

She lives in a large mansion on Bellview. Although I grew up in an upper middle-class home to the west of here, I'm certain I have never been inside such a splendid dwelling in my life.

"Are you absolutely certain?" she asks me again after we are seated across the room from each other.

"Have you committed murder? Robbed multiple banks?"

"No, but I doubt you could ever guess what I'm about to show you. You may faint dead away."

"Lay it on me." Although I say this with a smile, I'll admit I am already somewhat concerned.

There is an office just off the second living room. She goes there and soon rolls out a large dolly completely covered with computer paper boxes. I count eight of them. Seeing the boxes, I become more uneasy. She parks the load directly in front of me and returns to where she was sitting.

I glance over at her. I lift the cover of the first box and find the pages are in German. I flip through them ten pages at a time and, within less than a minute, I am convinced this is her large manuscript, already completed. I open a second box. English this time. The box begins with the title page. *The Prague Manuscript: Czech Crimes Against German and Hungarian Civilians, 1945-46.*

"The story is the same," she tells me. "Eight boxes. Four times 700 plus pages. English, German French, Czech. I paid translators in New York large sums of money for this work. And, Dr. Westbrook, did you really think I didn't know who led the Catholic forces at White Mountain that day? I was just testing you, to see if you were actually reading the pages I gave you."

I stare at the eight boxes. "When did you complete this massive work?"

"Four years ago. Of course, I had help. Anyway, as soon as I received my inheritance, I hired my three translators. I left the streets when I was 17 filled with despair. As soon as I began working on my manuscript, the feeling of despair evaporated and my thoughts became more organized."

"But the hostility remained." I gaze at her seriously. "Everly, I ask again, what are your plans for this large volume?"

She hesitates. "First, let me give you the source of my hostility. I ask you to listen carefully."

I watch her, captivated by her sense of sadness as she attempts to explain what happened to her family.

"My grandmother finally remarried when she was 23; my mother was born a year later. Things were still tough in Germany at that time, but the small family somehow muddled through. I never learned many of the financial details. No interest, I guess. A major problem arose when my grandmother's mental health began failing. Because she was brutally raped at age 16, she had always been fragile. Soon, she was beset by depression. Numerous physicians were approached, but none were able to help much. My grandmother eventually became convinced she was worthless. When my mother was nine, she came home from school one day to find my grandmother dead on the kitchen floor from a gun shot wound to the head. At the time they were living in the Bavarian town of Rosenheim, southeast of Munich."

"The situation now became critical. My mother's father, whose name is Kramar, had a brother who had immigrated to the United States and lived in Virginia. My mother and Kramar also immigrated to America as soon as possible. My mother finally met my own father in 1987." She laughs. "I was born in 1988."

"Well, the math works," I say, smiling a little.

"Of course. But the rest of my family's history is similarly tragic. My own father, the senator, also has a problem, though he hides it quite well."

"I've heard a few rumors."

"Exactly. I'm certain you've seen his photograph more than once in the papers. Extremely good looking. Women hound him. Unfortunately, I fear he encourages them."

"Where is your mother now?" My question seems to freeze her as still as a mannequin. After a few seconds her eyes come alive again.

"My mother is right here in Denver, in an institution. I visit her every other day. Some of the time she doesn't recognize me."

"I knew your parents were divorced. I had no idea what happened to your mother. And so, another reason for your present hostility."

"There were two reasons for my mother's collapse. My carousing father, often absent, and murdering and raping Czechs, whom I hold responsible for nearly everything!"

"The murdering Czechs are old men now, Everly, but please, on another point, do you realize until now I hadn't heard of Mr. Kramar, an actual blood relative."

She suddenly stiffens. "You let this rest! I mean it! Not another word!"

I suddenly catch my breath. Dear Jesus, I think, could the man possibly have been a child molester? If so, I cannot imagine women living under worse conditions. No wonder Everly's mother appears to be losing her mind. Everly continues to glare at me. I look away first, unable to withstand the penetrating power of those flashing green eyes. She eventually relaxes, and begins explaining the source of the facts on which she has relied.

"My facts were assembled by a retired professor from a university in Chicago," she explains. "I'll call Dr. Donner in advance and he can drive over to wherever you decide to drop me off. The two of us can then have a little chat. I haven't seen him for awhile."

"Sounds good." I gaze at her seriously. "Don't you blame Hitler at all? Remember, it was his invasion that eventually turned the Czech people against the Sudeten Germans."

"I really don't blame Hitler much for his occupation. It wasn't like Poland. The Czechs never had it so good as in that war. Hell, my research shows they were much better off than the Germans in Germany." She gives me a small smile. "Actually, I could sooner blame you than Hitler. I knew exactly what I was going to do the minute I viewed your little film. *Brothers at War* gave me a terrible kind of focus and, with the help of Professor Donner's facts, I began writing in a frenzy, rather like a member of some lunatic fringe!" I follow her eyes as they settle on the eight computer boxes in front of me.

"A great many words, probably all well-placed," I tell her.

"I prefer to think of those boxes as small atom bombs," she says.

Yes, 'little atom bombs'. I remember her statement as I lie here on my bed in my prison home, waiting for them to come at me again with a needle. But, for some reason, they do not bother me. Instead, what is bothering me at the moment is recalling Everly's account of her family's tragic history. I now understand more fully the source of her anger and disgust, especially considering the culprit was her own grandfather. No wonder Everly has issues!

I was also getting ready to consider the grandfather's name, Kramar, an actual blood relative, when my thoughts are suddenly interrupted by a stranger, standing silently in my doorway. He is a rather handsome man; tall, athletic looking, perhaps 40 years old, with white hair and blue eyes. Now he comes directly to my bed, offers his hand and introduces himself as Michael Novotny. I refuse to take his hand. He shrugs and sits down on a chair nearby. He is holding a clipboard, and has placed a couple of other items, books I think, on a small table over by my painted-over window.

"It is imperative that we talk," he tells me. "It will have to be now. You will address me as Mr. Novotny. By the way, I am told you attempted to escape last night."

"Yes, but I was caught. Your two soldiers were triumphant."

"My soldiers? I had never seen these men before this morning. Nor do I believe they are really soldiers. I don't know who they are." He is staring at me. "You planning some kind of action against my small country, Dr. Westbrook?"

"This statement has no meaning for me. I am a professor. I couldn't possibly have such power." But Everly might, I am thinking. Novotny does not seem dangerous at all. He does seem uneasy talking with me, though I can see he is trying to hide this.

I change the subject. "Hope you're not planning more torture, Mr. Novotny. My ass is still sore from the last injections." He eyes me strangely and for a few seconds neither of us speak. I have already decided I will lie like a common criminal if necessary to get through this interrogation. "Have I committed some serious crime, Mr. Novotny? Is this why I'm being detained here?"

"Are you considering a campaign against us sometime in the future? If so, you should know we are aware of everything you are doing; the many hundreds of pages which are ready for printing, the money you received from Illinois. Have you mailed this weighty manuscript to anyone else as yet? Listen! I am told this research of yours is a threat to central Europe and possibly the United States!"

For the moment I ignore these fanciful remarks. "You know, you speak perfect English with an American accent. Anyone listening might believe you really are American. Could you be CIA?"

He shakes his head and instead immediately comes back with his own forceful comments, first in perfect unaccented German, followed by something in a Slavic language, probably Czech. The German I understand easily. Translated loosely it is as follows: 'It can never be as it was during the middle of the last century. Don't ever think it! We will do everything possible to avoid such a political disaster'. As he spoke he had been watching me carefully. He appears to be calmer now. I wonder if he is thinking of the German invasion, or the communist occupation some years later. Surely the latter.

"I want us to turn to a few names and places," he continues. "I am told you have spoken all of these words yourself, in the night. I'm just trying to be honest with you."

"Honest, Mr. Novotny? What's honest about any of this? Why should I believe anything you say?" He looks at me sternly.

"Euro?" he says, ignoring my last remark.

I go along with this, though seeming to be confused. "Euro obviously has something to do with Europe. Can it be money?"

"Eger?"

"A town in the Sudetenland, Czecho-Slovakia. Hitler traveled through here in 1938."

"Ruth ?"

"A German lady I've known for several months."

"9-11, 2001?"

"This date means nothing to me," I say, lying again.

"Kriegsbaum?"

"I have never heard the name."

"Strange. You sent this man a friendly postcard less than six weeks ago."

"I remember nothing of this."

"Everly?"

I hesitate for a second or two. "One of my graduate students," I say finally.

"Where is the money, Dr. Westbrook?"

"I don't know. Maybe in Denver, or perhaps Everly has it. Of course, we had to have cash. I can't argue with that."

"Where is this Everly?"

"I wish I knew. I simply must locate her soon. I'm worried about her."

"We found your hotel room early this morning. We even paid your bill. We broke into your room safe. The manuscript was not there!" Novotny has become agitated again. "Where is your manuscript, Dr. Westbrook?"

Now I begin lying in earnest. "I have no idea. But had you not drugged me so heavily that first night, and quite possibly rammed my head into a pole, perhaps I could remember everything now." It seems he is shaking his head in astonishment at this statement. He finally continues, however.

"What special subject were you involved with, in order to write and soon print more than 700 pages of inflammatory propaganda?"

"I don't know, but you must have an inkling about it or you wouldn't be interrogating me like this. And if what I have written is mere propaganda, then surely you can successfully attack it."

"Kriegsbaum is dead. Hit and run." Novotny is smiling now. "How do you feel about this?"

"I feel nothing." I glance toward my painted-over window. "But hey, how about knocking open that window over there? Maybe then we could see some mountains."

He pays no attention. "After Kriegsbaum's death, his wife hurriedly took a plane to Bavaria. When we find her we'll know a lot more about your research." I only shake my head.

"Please answer everything orally and in a firm voice!"

"Understood," I say resignedly.

"The Eastern Front?"

I laugh aloud. "Mr. Novotny, my memory is perfect regarding World War Two. I could do an excellent job guiding you through the entire history of that war. Any European historian could do the same. The Eastern Front isn't our problem." Finally, he nods in agreement.

"The Czech Republic?"

More lying. "I have never heard of such a land."

"Jews?"

"I am not acquainted with many Jews. I suppose I think of them as many other non-Jews do. In my opinion, as a people they have suffered greatly."

"What did you understand from my small statement in German awhile ago?"

"I found it strange. According to what you told me, you seem to fear some approaching political disaster here in central Europe, one with which you believe I may be involved. Again, understand! I have no such connections! Now we've discussed many things this morning, but I still have no idea which side you are on." I grin at him.

"I am on the side of Europe and the United States of America," he says evenly. He slowly stands and stretches. He places his clipboard on the small table. I had already noticed he had brought along a couple of small hardcover books, which I imagine we will be dealing with later. Although we have not been at it long, Novotny seems tired. I am still convinced he is worried about something. Probably me.

"Break time, I believe," he says. "Want some coffee?" Now comes the good cop, I think.

"Sure, if it's hot. Tell them to send up some kolacky, too. I've always been fond of them." He nods in agreement and disappears into the hallway.

I remain there on my bed, contemplating everything Novotny has said thus far. A question is already bothering me. At what point do I announce I am not really the author of the fearsome *Prague Manuscript*, and throw all the weight on Everly's head. I smile broadly. Probably never. I have actually become quite fond of my young revolutionary, and would no doubt take a bullet for her. But I still plan to marry Ruth!

Ten minutes later Novotny is back, followed by a helper carrying a large tray with our coffee and kolacky. My God, just as I remembered; these cups really are big! I pick up a kolacky, hold it out, and then take a bite.

"My Czech heritage," I say, after swallowing.

"Westbrook is a pure English name."

"True, but in our neighborhoods in west Denver there was a mix of people; Czechs, Germans and others. These Czech kids, three or four generations removed from Europe, could still speak a little of the old language. One of them named me Vuscheck and told me it was my Czech name. My first girl friend when I was in the ninth grade was named Maria. Her parents were both Czech-Americans, at least as far as blood was concerned. But let's remember something: all of us kids were Americans, through and through, and our thoughts were practically never on the old countries in Europe." I pause and take a swig of coffee. "But don't ever try and turn me against my Czechs, Mr. Novotny. I am quite happy they have managed to hold onto their beautiful little land, along with their Slovak neighbors, of course."

"What do you mean, 'Slovak neighbors'?"

"I'm talking about Czechoslovakia," I answer, lying again.

"Well, a touching story, I suppose." He also takes a drink from his big coffee cup. "And are you still living in Denver, Colorado, teaching at a university there?"

"Yes, at least I was." I grab another kolaky." Boy, these things are good. A man could imagine he's, even now, right in the middle of Prague."

"Think so?"

"Yes. By the way, a lot of murders took place around here in 1945-46. Horror on a grand scale. Know anything about this?" He only stares at me. "Oh, and how's the Cold War coming along? Speak any Russian?"

"I am not a Russian specialist. Any Russian national would find my pronunciation crude." He goes for his coffee again; then his eyes harden slightly.

"Sudetenland?" he says.

I smile at him because this is one of my special subjects. "In western Czechoslovakia was a sort of rim around the edge on approximately three sides. This area was populated mostly by Germans before the end of the Second World War. As that war was winding down, a Czech leader named Eduard Benes gave a devastating speech in the city of Brno, encouraging Czechs to attack Germans and Hungarians and try and force them from the land. At the time there were more than 3,000,000 Germans there. Now I would guess there are a scant 60,000. Now, about the horror," I continue. "I expect the manuscript could give you the number, as well as the locations of the atrocities. Want to know the details, Mr. Novotny? Or are you afraid you wouldn't be able to sleep much afterward? This is no doubt my problem right now. I simply learned too much about the horror."

Novotny's eyes harden and he is glaring at me again. He is evidently determined to have a breakthrough with the man from Chicago. "Kriegsbaum!" he says harshly. "And please admit you knew him!"

I shake my head. "The first syllable of this word means 'war'. The second syllable means 'tree'. Perhaps if you stretched things just a bit you could come up with 'war tree', or 'tree of war'. You have referred to this man more than once. Do you think he's the person who gave me the money? And, by the way, how much did I get? I certainly hope Everly is not going hungry out there all by herself."

Novotny makes no comment about this. He seems to have given up on Kriegsbaum for the moment. "Why don't you finish your coffee?" he says. "I want you to look at some photographs." He takes one of the small books from the table and hands it to me. I take one last swig of coffee and am ready to follow his instructions.

I glance at the title page. "Slavic author; his work translated into German."

"Just the photographs, please. And any captions."

I begin turning the pages from front to back. Black and white photographs. German soldiers doing this or that, certainly nothing sinister I can see. Every time I am shown photographs of German soldiers, I think the person guiding me (in this case, Novotny) is trying to get me to come up with something bad! This photograph could be depicting soldiers from any occupying army, though in this case the officers are wearing German gray.

More soldiers, busy soldiers, trucks and jeeps around, no tanks. This photograph includes civilians along the edges. The German soldiers seem to be paying no attention to them. In another photograph are a few Russian soldiers. Now there are a couple of tanks off to the left. The caption under this photograph reads: SILESIA. No month or year is given, though I can imagine this could be part of the Soviet expansion into the west, perhaps toward the end of the war. A tiny sliver of Silesia is in the eastern part of what was the Sudetenland. The largest part, though, is in present-day Poland. Although I have heard plenty of evidence Russian soldiers committed atrocities at one time or another, I see no evidence of this here. Frankly, I don't know where Novotny is taking me with all this. This book seems to contain no photographs depicting scenes from the actual end of the war, or its aftermath. At no time have I seen the name 'Sudetenland' mentioned.

Novotny takes this book away and hands me a second one. This book is also by a Slavic author and is translated into German. More photographs. The first one jumps out at me. A German general is reviewing Czech troops. I know his name. He is Reinhard Heydrich. Novotny's hand is now on the photograph, stopping me from turning to the next page.

"Who is this man?" he asks me.

"His name is Heydrich, either a German general, or a high ranking Nazi official. This is the time after Hitler put him in charge of Bohemia and Moravia, an area known as the German Protectorate. This photograph was actually taken from 16 mm footage. In this footage Heydrich is walking along and the Czech troops are frozen in place, looking quite uneasy. The photograph is famous. Was Heydrich an evil man? I suppose it depends on your point of view. He was physically attractive, he played the violin, he truly loved his family, and I'm sure he loved Germany. But he was a Nazi to the core! I know he imprisoned many, and ordered at least hundreds killed. Were these victims Jews, intellectuals or criminals attacking elements of the German army? I'm afraid I don't know.

"Some have called him a monster. Was he? I cannot say. No doubt America killed a lot of innocent people in Vietnam, too. History is often complex and usually the winners write the history. But Heydrich was a Nazi! Of this there is no doubt. Czech commandos tracked him at the bidding of Mr. Benes, and Heydrich was a victim of a bomb attack. He died three days later. Because of this attack (the Germans would have called it an assassination), the Nazis razed the Czech village of Lidice, killed all the men and deported most of the women and children. The Czechs never forgot this outrage.

"Look, Mr. Novotny, as far as I know, I'm no authority on what happened in central Europe during the war and its aftermath. Without doubt many crimes were also committed against innocent German people, and the ancestors of some of those families had lived in these homes for hundreds of years. For example, I think I remember something terrible happened in a place called Aussig in the Sudetenland. Do you know anything about this?" I see the little finger of his left hand suddenly flies up partway.

But Novotny does not answer me. He takes the book from my hands. "This is all we need," he says. "I was only interested in your reaction to the photograph of Heydrich." He hesitates for a few seconds and then takes a deep breath. "You know, Dr. Westbrook, I continue to be puzzled about you. Some of your statements and your reactions seem unbelievable in light of what we know about the research you have conducted. If I did not know those incendiary 700 pages had been written, so help me God, I would offer you my hand and simply let you walk out of this place."

"Good, then let's halt this nonsense and the two of us go out and enjoy a few strong Czech beers!"

Novotny ignores this, of course. A slight hesitation. "You do wish to regain your memory, do you not?"

"I would like that very much," I say. "Unless, of course, all the horrible memories from the past came together and eventually drove me insane." I gaze at him evenly. "And the drugs you are giving me are not helping the situation. A few times I believe I came close to dying."

"Drugs? What drugs? Until this morning I had no idea an American professor was being kept in this broken-down home. And I certainly had nothing to do with the administering of any drugs. I've listened to the tape of your utterances, of course. On the way over here actually."

"Then who. . ."

"I am not certain, but I intend to find out. I have a feeling a certain segment of the power structure here in this city is about to be carefully scrutinized. I only hope no other innocent civilians will be harmed in the meantime. But we still have a major disagreement, Dr. Westbrook. I need to examine your manuscript. Why don't you just produce it and save us both a lot of trouble?"

"This is impossible. I don't know where it is."

"Well, I can't do anything about your situation at the moment, but when I come back later with more authority we'll see about getting you out of here. Meanwhile, don't worry about any additional harassment. I've already put a stop to it. You may be surprised to learn there are even some in my own police department who defend those in charge here. Why they do it is beyond my comprehension." He observes me seriously for a few seconds; then he stands and walks from the room, this time without offering me his hand.

Novotny was partially correct. I really had received an extremely large donation from an old German gentleman who was interested in our research. But I had not lied to Novotny in this instance. The old donor had refused to give his name. I have no reason to believe his name was Kriegsbaum.

Everly and I were on a plane the second day after the meeting at her home, where I first viewed the eight boxes of her manuscript (English, German, French, and Czech). By the time we landed in Chicago it was snowing. We rented a car at O'Hare and then I dropped her off at a mall near Lake Forest, where supposedly she will meet with her old friend, Professor Donner. I go on, looking for a particular mansion which, after driving around for awhile, I find almost hidden behind several large fir trees. I first park in the street, but almost immediately a young man of perhaps 30 walks down the lane toward me through the gently falling snow. He explains he will open the gate, and I should drive inside. Because of his accent, I know immediately he is German. He guides me inside the mansion itself and then into a large, beautifully furnished room where the fire in the fireplace is burning brightly. Within minutes I hear the gently humming sound of a lift from somewhere high in the house. I remember the sound had blended nicely in counterpoint with the crackling of the fire. A few seconds later the young German servant opens a door and the master of the house joins me on crutches. My opinion at the time was that he could be close to 90 years old. I stand and he meets me in the center of the large room and, leaning on just one crutch, offers his hand. Although I am hoping all goes well with our meeting, I will admit I was prepared to lie as often as necessary. I will also admit that, more than once, I have been bothered by this dishonesty, remembering I have not written one word of the manuscript. I imagine I've been influenced to a great extent by Everly, who seems not to be bothered by any underhandedness in which one might indulge from time to time.

"Dr. Westbrook? As David told you on the phone, I have learned a great deal about you. How goes the manuscript?" I watch as with great difficulty he seats himself in a rather high, adequately stuffed chair not far from the fire. Something about his eyes bother me, though perhaps it is only his advanced age I am noticing.

"Everything is going well, Sir," I tell him. "Your gift will help a great deal as I make my final trip to the Czech Republic. Of course, most of the manuscript is already complete. I trust I was clear about this to David on the phone."

"Quite clear indeed. We do, however, still need to discuss a few minor points. I am hoping you have half an hour or so."

"I have as much time as you wish, Sir. I do want to stress once again, however, if your financial gift went directly to my university in Denver, it could provide a tax-deduction for you or your company."

"We will discuss this aspect a bit later. First of all, at what point in the history of this travesty of justice do you plan to begin your story?" I still notice a slight German accent, but otherwise his command of the English language is perfect.

"*The Prague Manuscript* presents much of the history of Czechoslovakia, however, your interest will probably begin when Adolf Hitler enters the Sudetenland in 1938."

"Let's just call him 'Hitler', shall we? I would rather our discussion dispenses with niceties such as his first name."

I nod in agreement. "From 1938 until the end of the war in 1945, I plan to bring out any major Nazi atrocities I discovered, as well as acts of terror against the German army, the Wehrmacht, and those administering the Protectorate. Of course, we cannot ignore the concentration camp at Theresienstadt. As you know, many people were imprisoned there. Finally, we turn to Czech crimes against German and Hungarian civilians. There were many thousands of them, extending long after the war was over." At this point I am grimacing.

"What is your opinion of Eduard Benes?"

"He loved his homeland, but he had persuaded himself that the German people living there were all Nazi sympathizers, or worse! His speech in Brno at the end of the war was an abomination, as were his several decrees, which have supposedly been in effect for more than 60 years." I smile. "Of course, except for two or three decrees, no one pays much attention to them these days."

"Can the actions of Benes be explained logically in any way?"

"Only in terms of power politics. Keeping the Czechs stirred up was his only hope of attaining power after the war, and this includes the bombing of Reinhard Heydrich in 1942, which Benes instigated from England. Of course, I can't defend Heydrich much myself."

"Would you care for some coffee, Dr. Westbrook?" the old man asks, breaking into the conversation again. He pulls some cord I had not seen, even before I answer him.

"Of course," I say, smiling. "A cup of coffee is sometimes helpful as one wrestles with gigantic themes." I look at him more closely now. His full head of white hair is combed straight back in the style many men preferred at about the halfway point in the 20th century or before. Although he is crippled now, I can imagine a powerful physique in play in earlier years.

"Would you like to tell me something about yourself?" I ask him. "You already know so much about me. Surely you were a soldier."

He nods slowly. "My unit was as far to the south and east as were any German soldiers in the war. We were attempting to break through to the oil in the Caucasus. It was there my legs were shot out from under me." A sad smile is now playing around his lips. "I spent the rest of the war behind a desk, though still in the East."

The coffee and small pieces of cake arrive then and we are each provided with a tray. We are served by the same young German I have seen once before. "And your family?" I ask politely.

"My young wife died in Dresden. We had no children."

"I'm sorry," I say, already wishing to heaven I had avoided the subject.

He meets my eyes. "It was a long time ago. Many hideous decisions were made in that war. The killing of the Jews and the fire bombing of Dresden were two of the most glaring here in central Europe." He takes a swig of coffee from an exquisite antique cup, exactly like the one I myself am holding.

"And you, Dr. Westbrook, are you married?"

"Not yet, though my German fiancee and I are planning to marry some-time in the near future. She is from Munich."

He nods. We are both silent for a few seconds.

"I have one more major question for you, Dr. Westbrook. Give me your honest opinion as to how *The Prague Manuscript* will affect the people of the Czech Republic."

This is easy. All I need to do is quote from my documentary film of five years ago. "If what I have discovered is published, as I'm certain it will be, it really will have a negative impact on that small nation." I eye him seriously. "Of course, the Germans have been forced to chew on the truth for decades now. I think it is only fitting the Czechs do their own bit of chewing for awhile. The power of our manuscript lies in the fact that I have knowledge of many of the atrocities which were committed there in 1945-46."

"But we had occupied their land since 1939. Can one blame them for reacting negatively?"

"Perhaps it is a mistake for me to be so outspoken, but I feel I have to lay this aspect out forcefully. Forgive me, Sir, but are you certain you really know what happened in the Sudetenland at the end of the war? Because I can assure you many thousands of innocent Germans died there at the time. Many Hungarians were killed as well. Also, everything both groups had owned was stolen from them."

"I imagine you are correct in this assessment, and I would guess you and your fiancee are about to let the entire world know about these atrocities. I am trusting my gift will help with the publication and promotion of your large manuscript." He smiles at me now, and for an instant looks about 30 years younger.

"We were going to discuss a tax-deduction for you," I remind him then.

His head tilts ever so slightly toward the right, almost as though this might help him phrase the wording of his next paragraph. "I am ill, Dr. Westbrook. My physician gives me six months at most. Therefore, any thought of a tax-deduction would be a waste of time. No, I will give you my donation in cash. David!" he calls. "The suitcase, please!" He turns back to me again. "Don't bother counting it. I imagine it will be enough. If it isn't, please reach me by phone. Of course, you dare not wait too long to do this." He smiles.

"But, Sir, do you realize I don't even know your name?"

"Right, and you don't need to know it, either!" He laughs aloud. "I won't bother standing." He offers his hand from his chair. I take his hand and give him my thanks.

"Good luck, my young friend. Please be careful and remember, the world is filled with evil, lying people." The young German named David hands me a small suitcase and I am escorted from the room and the mansion. He follows me to my car.

"Do not feel guilty about the large amount of money in your suitcase," he says. "My benefactor no longer needs it. Within three months he will be gone. Soon after that I will be gone also, to South America. He has been very good to me." We shake hands and he opens the gate. I wave to him and drive away through the gently falling snow.

I immediately retrieve Everly and we return to O'Hare International and arrange to keep our rental car overnight and then drop it off in Denver tomorrow afternoon. Dr. Donner had already left and so I did not have a chance to meet him. No matter. I have other things on my mind. The suitcase containing the uncounted funds is already in the trunk of our car. We agree it will be better to wait until we stop at a motel somewhere in Nebraska to count the money. Everly takes the first turn at the wheel and, while heading toward the Quad Cities on Highway 80, I give her a detailed account of my meeting with the old soldier.

"He will eventually be watching the mail for his copy of *The Prague Manuscript*," I tell her.

"It doesn't matter. We'll wait a month and then send him a copy of the large German version. Your name, as well as the university's name, will be on the title page. It will make him happy, and I can't see there is any downside. A reminder: I told you we probably would not be returning to Denver by plane. Can you imagine what would have happened had we attempted to shove that suitcase full of cash through inspections in the airport? By the way, what did you think of this man? Did he give you his name?"

"No name. But actually, I liked him. I imagine he was a good soldier, though what his duties were in connection with that desk assignment toward the end of the war, I have no idea." I take a deep breath. "We discussed Benes and the decrees."

"Naturally. Well, to hell with Benes! And now, how much money do you think is in that suitcase there in the trunk? Not that I want any of it."

I laugh. "Then why should you care? Considering your net worth you will probably think it's a piddling amount regardless." I glance out the window at the consistently flat landscape. "Everly, I've been wondering about your reaction two nights ago at your home, when I mentioned Mr. Kramar. Had he done something to you? It is what I thought."

She hesitates. "He had been molesting my mother for years, and he was already after me! Of course, soon after we moved to Denver, my mother was safe in a mental institution. My own father, who could have protected me, was seldom around. Why in hell do you think I took to the streets? Old Grandpa Kramar, naturally. I know he finally had to run to Central America. I hope he's dead!"

"Is he Czech or German, Everly?" But she only glares at me, and so I shut up.

Just before we reached the Quad Cities, we stopped for a ten minute break, and afterward I took the wheel. By the time we crossed the Mississippi River she is curled up asleep against her door.

I watch her sometimes, especially when lights strike her face. She looks like an innocent 13-year-old resting there, but I know this impression is false. Her plan for revenge must already be in its advanced stages, though thus far she has not shared any of the details. But I know she intends to carry out this plan. For me, it is unnerving.

I envision her standing alone at some high place there in central Europe, perhaps looking down at the Moldau River and the ancient city of Prague. The borders are all fixed now, and it is mostly quiet on the eastern front, yet I fear there could still be one bullet left for her. But until now I was unable to fully comprehend what had brought Everly to this dangerous juncture. It is not just a country Everly is at odds with; it is her second grandfather, a child molester on the lam, who just happens to be Czech!

After one last stop near Council Bluffs, we pound on as far as York, Nebraska, where we finally pull in for the night. We get a single room with two beds because Everly refuses to stay alone in a second room. I lay the suitcase on her bed. "Go ahead and count it," I tell her. "I trust you." I watch as she carefully leafs through some of the money in the upper tier.

"They're all thousand dollar bills."

"Impressive! So, get a final count and then place the suitcase in between our beds up toward your reading light." I head to the bathroom to put on my pajamas.

"$1,900,000," she tells me a few minutes later. Her face is serious. "Quite a bit more than we thought."

"Well, with master criminals such as ourselves on the loose, what can you expect?" I say this even though I still feel guilty about lying to the old soldier.

"We are not criminals! There is not one word in our large manuscript we didn't write ourselves!"

"So, you are including *Brothers at War* in the mix?"

"Of course! The only creative thinker present in this small room right now is you! I'm a better writer and I'm fast as lightning, but to tell you the truth, I don't believe I've ever had one creative thought in my entire life! Like the Japanese, who copy all things German, I have copied you. Of course, I didn't know at the time you were going to turn out to be such a nice guy." She tosses her pajamas over her right shoulder and heads for the bathroom. I hear her laughing as she turns on the water.

I kill my bedside light and within minutes I find myself falling asleep. I have been up since four a.m., and I'm guessing it's sometime after midnight now. Everly has been quite restless, actually as though talking with someone. I've tried to ignore it. It must have been almost one o'clock when I feel her snuggling close to me in my small bed. "Sorry," she tells me. "I was just cold, and sort of lonely." She gives me a quick kiss on my left shoulder. I smile there in the darkness, and when I do finally go back to sleep, I am holding her hand.

When I awake the next morning, she is already in the shower. She soon comes out with a towel wrapped around her. We give each other friendly smiles and I go into the bathroom and turn on the water to shave. Later, dressed and ready for breakfast, I take the small suitcase with us. Sitting across from each other there in the restaurant, I discuss my plans for the money. I tell her I am going to visit my bank and rent a rather large safety deposit box. I ask again if she might not change her mind and take half the money herself. She shakes her head and changes the subject.

"Dr. Westbrook, this will be the last time you ever hear the polite form of your name, unless, of course, we are with others. From now on, you are 'Bob'. Okay?"

"Sure, it makes sense. There should always be familiarity as well as honor among thieves." I grin at her. "It's been quite a ride since that day in January when I first met you. I remain astonished at what you've accomplished since you were 17. But I still have doubts about those months when you were, as you said, running loose on the streets. I'll bet you smoked some pot, drank some beer, and slept with a couple of guys. Please don't answer. I enjoy thinking of you as being sort of innocent." She shrugs and continues smiling at me. We finish our breakfast, go back to our room to pack, and then drive away, heading west.

We are less than 100 miles outside of Denver, coming down from Ogallala, Nebraska on Highway 76, when Everly's phone rings. I'm driving and so she can get at it immediately. Well, it turns out to be the big cheese, President Harald Haverkamp. He suggests that a meeting be held this afternoon. Everly opts for four o'clock. When I look at the dash clock I see it is already after one-thirty. I soon learn from Everly's side of the conversation that Haverkamp is requesting my presence at this meeting. He must have also asked Everly if she knows where I am, and Everly, who I'm certain doesn't give a damn, tells the president I am sitting right here next to her. When the president requests a conversation with me, she answers: "I will certainly ask him." By now I am looking out the left window laughing to myself. I eventually reach for the phone. "Good afternoon, President Haverkamp. I hear you've scheduled a meeting. No, four o'clock should work fine. Would you mind giving me a general sense of the agenda?"

"Travel possibilities regarding the end of the semester," he tells me. I say 'okay' and hand the phone back to Everly. This time she is on the phone a relatively long time. When she finally signs off she is quiet for several seconds.

"Something amiss?" I ask.

"Actually, something strange. A publishing company named the Bohemian Central Press in Prague is interested in publishing our large manuscript. They would like to meet with me sometime in the spring."

"So, what's the problem? I should think you would be overjoyed."

"I'm puzzled about something. You see, I've never approached them about my writing. How did this company find out about me?"

"Well, I don't believe the print media had anything to do with it. Your name disappeared from the original article as soon as it reached Chicago. Have you ever discussed your writing on television?"

She shakes her head. "What did Haverkamp say to you?"

"He said something about travel possibilities later in the semester. I can't understand what any of this has to do with me. In spite of what I told the old soldier in Lake Forest, I have no plans to return to Europe this spring. As far as I know, Ruth is still planning to visit me in Colorado early in the summer. Now, about the meeting, I assume it's in President Haverkamp's office."

She nods. "You know, Bob, your film, my thesis, and the large manuscript are the only things that connect us. This has to be the reason they invited you to the meeting. They know nothing about the Lake Forest donation." She shakes her head, somewhat in frustration. "Things seem to be moving rather fast right now."

"You are certainly correct about that," I answer.

Closer to Denver we leave Highway 76 and turn onto E-470, heading to the airport to drop off our rental. I had picked Everly up early yesterday morning to catch our plane, and so my own car is there waiting for us. I take Everly home and tell her I'll see her at the meeting. I have been in a bad mood ever since she mentioned that publishing company in Prague. I wish I could keep her from going there. Glancing at the dash clock, I see I still have time to get rid of the money. I drive directly to my bank on County Line Road and lock away those thousand dollar bills. After finishing this chore, I feel a little better. Naturally.

Although Everly seemed not to have grasped the reason for the four o'-clock meeting, I am quite certain I understand what the administration is up to. They want to pay my expenses to accompany my revolutionary graduate student to the Czech Republic. My God, I think, surely not alone! But, with this administration, one never knows. I can even imagine Vice President O'Roark joining us at the meeting, arguing I should become involved in their plan.

I'm already torn as to what to do about the situation with the travel. On the one hand, I would rather be the one who accompanies Everly overseas if need be. Yet a part of me would prefer she not go at all. Of course, I have a strong personal interest in the meeting this afternoon, which has nothing to do with Everly. I feel I need to see Ruth again as soon as possible, and it is conceivable the university is getting ready to cut me some slack this spring regarding my schedule. I decide to take things as they come.

When I walk into the meeting about one minute late, I find President Haverkamp, Vice President O'Roark, and Everly sitting around in a large circle. I notice there are two extra chairs. I choose a chair opposite Everly and sit down. Everly gives me a smile, but O'Roark and Haverkamp merely nod. The two administrators have never been fond of me. I am a staunch Republican, while they side more often with professors leaning toward the socialist realm. I do not have a great many friends on this campus. Many of those teaching here, I would love to fire! It will not surprise me if one day I see a mammoth statue being erected, in either Denver or Boulder, in the like-ness of Karl Marx! For all I know, there may be one already.

The vice president begins the conversation. "Dr. Westbrook, our first question relates to Ms. Somerset's thesis. What are the chances it could be finished in time for her to graduate in the late spring or early summer?"

I don't even hesitate. "The chances are excellent. I believe we can count on it." At that moment the door opens and Haverkamp's secretary ushers a fourth man into the room. I recognize him at once. It is Senator Charles Somerset, billionaire politician, and father of Everly. I am introduced, and he shakes the hands of the males, but only nods toward his daughter. Her face is noncommittal.

Their plan has now become clear to me. Hoping to gain favor with his daughter, the senator has somehow learned the name of a tame publishing house in Prague, laid several thousand on those in charge, and received the promise of them publishing a book in return. Wait until the Czech company learns that the manuscript is 700 pages plus! But few companies in the western world would agree to publish a manuscript sight unseen, not without receiving payment in advance. And I am certain no one in the Czech Republic has ever seen Everly's book, because all pages are either in her mansion in Denver, snug in my own office at the university, or locked away somewhere here in Prague. This means the Bohemian Central Press has already been presented with a rather nice check.

The Senator is looking at me now. "The thesis appears to be quite an undertaking."

You have no idea, I think. I glance at Everly. I'm not certain how much information she wants to share. As I watch her, I'm feeling a certain amount of unease. But she fearlessly plows ahead. "My thesis is approximately 160 pages long. However, you should all realize the thesis is actually a portion of a much larger work, which is well over 700 pages in length. It is the larger work I will eventually publish. My interest in the M.A. program is secondary."

I see this news has shaken the Senator. O'Roark and Haverkamp appear totally confused. "Ms. Somerset," O'Roark finally asks in frustration, "are we to understand that you, at the age of 22, have completed an undergraduate degree and all of the course work for an M.A. degree, and have also written a manuscript of more than 700 pages in length, all accomplished since you were 17?"

"And all accomplished with a four point average," I put in.

Total silence. O'Roark and Haverkamp stare at each other. "Of course," Haverkamp finally injects, "we are naturally mainly concerned with the thesis. I believe we can leave the details to Ms. Somerset and her advisor."

"Of course," O'Roark echoes. "Perhaps now we can turn our attention to a few other matters. Such as travel." The Vice President has turned to me again. "How does your schedule look toward the beginning of April, Dr. Westbrook?"

I'm not the least bit surprised by the question, but I hold back, pretending to be noncommittal. "I have approximately 250 undergraduate history students. By the middle of April we will be conducting massive reviews for final exams. It is a tension-filled time of year, a time when many students look to their instructors for assistance."

For several seconds it is deathly quiet there in the president's spacious office. The three males are shifting around in their chairs just a little. Everly is watching me with intense interest, though surely, she knows what the next question will be. The two administrators are about to stray over the line and I'm enjoying every minute of their unease. I am even smiling a little.

"We are developing a few ideas," Haverkamp tells us. He is watching me carefully. "I suggest you give your final exams early this semester. Give your undergraduates a choice. They can either accept the grade they have at that time, or take a rather simple cognitive final which, as I just stated, will be given much earlier than usual." All eyes are on me now, as they wait to see if I'm about to bow to university pressure. I already know what they are going to ask. I just want to make them sweat a little.

"I have heard of such practices before. I am just not certain about such an educational plan for our students. It rather seems as though we are gypping them!"

"Let's cut to the chase here!" O'Roark says firmly. I notice his chin is sort of sticking out, and that his voice has risen to a higher pitch than usual. "You are a young associate professor, only recently on tenure! I should think you would be happy to cooperate with us regarding this matter!"

"You haven't yet asked me to do anything special," I answer, "except relax my standards at the end of the present semester." I scan the three men's faces. "Why don't you just tell me what you want?"

But now the senator is stirring slightly. I'm waiting for him to clarify the situation. My Lord, he's a handsome individual! I can understand why certain women are after him.

"I am perhaps at fault here," he begins. "For some time I have been interested in providing my daughter with an exceptional educational experience. I understand her thesis deals with the Czech Republic. I am also acquainted with Dr. Westbrook's film, *Brothers at War*." He looks at me now. "Because I consider you to be highly knowledgeable about the countries of central Europe, I should greatly appreciate it if you would consider accompanying my daughter to Prague, not only to further her education generally, but also to help her attain a greater appreciation of Bohemian culture."

Now we hear from Everly! "Father, why in hell are you discussing me in the third person? And thus far you've scarcely looked at me! So typical! And did you really think I wouldn't know who bought off the Bohemian Central Press? Good God!"

"Everly, Everly!" Well, he's certainly looking at her now! "I thought this trip might be a kind of gesture on my part, something that might eventually bring us together. The past has often not been pretty. Your one grandfather, killed in the war, your grandmother, a hopeless suicide, a second grandfather missing, and now, your own mother! I am hoping a trip back to that ancient land might bring about a change of perspective on your part. People often change, Everly. The Czech people today have nothing to do with their ancestors, who lived back there at the end of the war."

We can sure as hell hope not, I think, considering what I fear Everly has in store for them!

"Why the change of heart, Father? You had no interest in me when I was younger, leaving me in the care of an illegal weakling from Guatemala, who I turned into my slave when I was ten! And you have the nerve to bring up my mother? Well, you can share a lot of the blame for her present condition! You're damned lucky I blame the Czechs more!"

Haverkamp jumps in immediately, attempting to restore some civility into the discussion. "Now the university would cover all expenses of the trip," he says rather loudly. "Up to $10,000."

"How long would we be gone?" I ask, thinking the money doesn't impress me much, as I had just locked away nearly $2,000,000 an hour ago.

"About 15 days. We think that would be sufficient time. Ms. Somerset could then graduate sometime in the early summer."

It is then I bring up something a great many people would have been considering several minutes ago. "I am 32 years old. Everly is a beautiful girl of 22." I smile at her. "Even in this new century, society usually frowns on associate professors who run off with their graduate students."

"Yes, but we know about your Czech girl friend who lives in Munich," O'Roark puts in. "We assume the two of you would spend some time visiting her. Perhaps she could even accompany you when you travel to the Czech Republic."

"Ruth Wedemeyer is not Czech. By blood and culture she is German." Somebody has been scanning my e-mails, I think. I wonder why the three are so anxious to get Everly and me on our way. I mean, why not put it off until later in the summer after Everly has graduated? Perhaps they are concerned I have other plans for the summer. Or perhaps, like Hitler, who just couldn't wait to invade the Soviet Union, they decided the time for action is now!

"Dr. Westbrook, how do you feel about our idea?" This, of course, from Senator Somerset.

"It is up to Everly. I'll make the trip if she is interested in going." I am watching her now. Her face is steady, determined, patient. But I know inside she is still feeling deep antagonism. When she finally speaks, she is like a robot.

"I should very much like to visit all areas of the Czech Republic," she tells us, causing me to shudder slightly.

And that statement basically marked the end of the meeting; in fact, the others had seemed rather satisfied with the result. But they don't know half of what I know, and I was strongly tempted to tell them a few things. But instead, I gave Everly a friendly nod and then left for home to write another long e-mail to Ruth. It is after one o'clock in Europe. Far too late to call. I feel certain Ruth had accepted the new position in Berlin, though she had been telling me recently she still wants us to somehow get together in the spring or early summer. Of course, she has no idea I will already be in Europe in just a few short weeks. My e-mail will bring her up-to-date about this. Looking back, I believe Everly and I must have flown from Denver to Munich sometime in April. I am no longer certain about the exact date.

Ruth was the one person giving the university cover for my trip with Everly. Without Ruth, Everly and I might already have become romantically involved. Of course, I doubt that either Haverkamp or O'Roark would have cared. Their only goal would have been keeping the massive donations from Everly's father flowing into the university at a steady pace.

I remain in my small prison room, waiting for a man named Novotny, who I am still confident will be coming by to rescue me. My mind has been wandering for several minutes, and by now it must be almost twelve o'clock. I notice a young woman standing in my doorway.

"You have two visitors in the cafeteria," she tells me in accented English. I had seen this girl on several occasions. A time or two she had even brought food into my room. But until this moment I have never heard her speak one word of either German or English. And so, it would seem the nasty woman in charge of this facility is running a tight ship.

I am convinced the second person down in the cafeteria is Everly. I take the stairs this time, trusting I will never need to use the big lift again. The stairs are deserted. Few of the older people ever use them. When Everly sees me, she stands and throws her arms around me and kisses me on the cheek. I know I am grinning like a crazy person, but I can't help it. It would be difficult to explain my exact feelings at this moment but, suffice to say, I am overjoyed to see Everly again.

I nod to Novotny and then the two of us join him at his table. I think he may have been surprised that my greeting with Everly was not more demonstrative. I imagine he was under the impression she is my girl friend. Just before hugging me she had thrown me a wink, letting me know I am still supposed to cover for her regarding the manuscript.

Both Everly and Novotny are interested in what I can remember. I lie, slowly shaking my head. "Practically nothing. I'm certain I will eventually find the manuscript, but they kept me so full of drugs here I can barely remember recent history. Tell me again how you learned of our research?" I ask Novotny.

"Kriegsbaum, of course. You will remember we spoke of this man earlier this morning. Some people here are insisting he mailed a check of $75,000 to you in Colorado, with the promise of another $50,000 when your research is published. I've heard this Kriegsbaum actually brags about the grant. It is said he even wrote an article about the process in a German magazine. I can't believe you do not remember this man."

"I'm sorry, but I don't believe anyone named Kriegsbaum promised me money. Nor do I remember any check." It is absolutely amazing, I am thinking, how certain people in this city are scrambling the facts of this case. And Novotny seems to be buying into some of it. I watch him carefully as he continues.

"My own chief of police late yesterday afternoon told me the F.B.I. has been interested in Mr. Kriegsbaum for some time, because of certain right-wing views he shares with a small minority of German citizens." He glances at Everly, and then back at me. "But look, I have no interest in the money this man paid you. All my government wants is to briefly take possession of the 700 pages of research, and then perhaps persuade you not to publish them."

I smile. "You sure you aren't just planning to nab the manuscript, Mr. Novotny?"

I think I see Everly frowning from the corner of my eye. "Frankly, Bob, the U.S. State Department also has a negative view of our research, though I imagine this may stem from the source of the money. By the way, you've never told me about receiving any donation."

Good Lord, she's really running with it! What a faker! I ignore her words and turn my attention back to Novotny. "You have never read our completed research. At present, because of my memory loss, I can't defend it myself, but what if our stated results are true? Would you just have us toss everything?"

"I would!" he says emphatically. He hesitates for a second or two. "I am Czech. I feel I have a good understanding of what has been written because of what your girl friend told me this morning, and from what Kriegsbaum has written earlier. Frankly, I fear your manuscript could damage the Czech Republic should it ever be published."

"I thought we were talking about Czechoslovakia," I remark, lying again.

"Czechoslovakia is no more," Everly says with a smile. "We can discuss this later as your memory begins to return. I also learned the present German government is against the publication of our manuscript. And yes, I've been visiting with them, too. I was doing everything I could to find you, Bob." I am now shaking my head in disbelief. Such statements seem outlandish to me. Before Everly and I were considering coming to Europe, I was under the impression practically no one outside the United States had ever heard of us. I notice Everly is looking seriously at Novotny.

"Now we are in agreement! Correct? The American government wants Dr. Westbrook released immediately. And you know as well as I do that it is against European law to keep him prisoner here. We have already discussed this."

"We will release him, but I really need to see the manuscript. Where in hell is this monster work? You know, even as we speak, my colleagues are searching your room in your new hotel. Does this worry you, Miss Everly?"

"No, but I hope they don't make a mess." (Everly may not be worried, but I am. I am convinced a certain key is somewhere on her person at this very moment!)

"You know," she tells Novotny, "Bob's memory will soon return and we will locate the manuscript. When that happens, we will drop it by your office and you can make a copy if you like."

Novotny is shaking his head in frustration. He seems uncertain as to what to do next. But we are interrupted at that moment by the team I have already seen before, the middle-aged man and woman, who I believe may be in charge of the two soldiers with whom I have been sparring. Their eyes are on Novotny and they begin their tirade in Czech while still ten feet away. Although I cannot understand a word, I imagine they are vehemently arguing that I should not be released.

"Who in hell are these losers?" Everly asks me. "So help me God, if they try and stop us from leaving here, I suggest we stomp both of them! Perhaps

Mr. Novotny will help us." Novotny holds up his left hand, motioning for peace and quiet. The man and woman by now are standing beside our table, waving their arms around and basically raising hell. Novotny immediately demands quiet and looks at Everly and me again. "You may leave," he tells us quietly. "Enough is enough. If your big book should turn up, I would naturally like to glance at it." The two of us wish him well and head out toward the hallway which leads to the main door.

"Oh, just one more thing." He is calling to us. "It is rather silly, but I practically never get a chance to laugh at my own history. It is something many Germans say. They say: 'Those crazy Czechs! They always throw their best people out the window'!" Everly and I both laugh along with him, though I must admit my own mind has not yet caught up with his joke. I'm certain it will eventually come to me. We wave to him again and leave the cafeteria. I noticed the two strangers had taken our places at the table, no doubt ready for a massive confrontation.

The Mercedes I had rented a week ago in Germany is parked on the street, a beautiful silver-colored automobile which would tempt any thief in the world. I had already nearly forgotten what it looked like. It is not until I am approaching the passenger side door that I see the massive damage; three large indentations, two just behind the door and one on the door itself. Whatever had caused the damage must have had something to do with red paint because this color is in evidence along the edges of each of the indentations. I call to Everly who, after looking over the situation, states the damage had to have occurred in the last half hour, while she was meeting me in the home. She tells me she had walked by this side of the car in the deep garage at her hotel, just before driving out into the street and coming here. At that time, she insists, there was no damage.

"What do you think could have done this?" I ask her. "My guess is a sledge hammer dipped in red paint."

Everly is still staring at the car. "It seems like rage to me. We have German plates here, from Mannheim actually, but surely this wouldn't have mattered to anyone. There are cars with German plates all over this city. But it sure seems somebody was mad as hell!"

"Pop the hood if you don't mind, Everly. My thoughts are probably turning fanciful, but I need to check for something else." Finding nothing wrong under the hood, I drop down to the pushup position and examine the car's underbelly from all four sides.

"You're looking for a bomb," she says.

"There is no bomb," I say, rising to my feet again. "I guess we are back to considering rage as our motive. Let's drive to your new hotel." I am finally able to smile and relax a little. "You know, except for the silver color, this is just like my own Mercedes back in Denver."

"That is probably why we chose it. But Mr. Novotny told me one must be careful here. Criminals can evidently differentiate between rentals and other run-of-the-mill vehicles. To be perfectly honest, I did not feel safe driving to the airport that first night. And I swear, one of those powerful BMWs, a black one, tailed me right up to where I turned into the terminal with the boxes of our manuscript. Thankfully, I didn't see the car again while returning to the hotel."

As soon as we are driving away she glances over at me. "I've been in touch with Ruth. She will be back in her Munich apartment in a couple of days. She has been worried sick because she didn't hear from you."

"But I guess she did take the new job in Berlin."

"Yes, but I think she may already be regretting the decision. At first she thought Berlin was an exciting place, and figured you could join her there just as easily as in Munich. But living in that huge city, she soon realized it was filled with hundreds of thousands of foreigners who had not the slightest interest in German culture, or learning the German language. Frankly, I expect her to be coming back to Munich permanently. I've spoken with her by phone four times. I got her number by hacking into some of your e-mails."

"I've really missed her!"

"That's understandable." She hesitates a couple of seconds. "Bob, I have a meeting scheduled for tomorrow at four o'clock with an editor at the Bohemian Central Press. I'd like you to join me. You are appearing on the title page as co-author."

"I'll be happy to go with you tomorrow. Just as long as I can get back to Munich in time to meet Ruth."

"No problem. That's three days from now."

"Okay. You know, Everly, I'm still trying to figure out who was behind my abduction. I'm certain the man and woman back there were involved, but they can't be at the decision-making level. Novotny insists he had nothing to do with what happened, and I believe him. I think he suspects people higher up in the city government were involved, though that seems a stretch."

"Was it true people were drugging you back there to keep you immobile? Novotny said you told him that." We have stopped for a red light now and, during this tiny interval, I check my side mirror. I am happy to see there is no black BMW behind us. The light changes and we drive on.

"They gave me the needle on at least three occasions. And for all I know, they were slipping drugs into my food occasionally. Last night I tried to escape, but two soldier types caught me and returned me to my room. I was obviously weaker then than I thought. I'll bet you didn't know I was in a wheelchair sometimes during the first three days."

"You're kidding!"

"No, at the beginning it was bad! I still have trouble remembering everything. So, the manuscript is in a locker in the airport?"

"Yes." She glances over at me. "Now, Bob, there are other matters to discuss. When I couldn't find you after a couple of days, I called the university and got in touch with Haverkamp. He admitted he had been glancing through your e-mails almost daily, trying to follow our itinerary. When I spoke with him he appeared quite anxious. You know, I didn't realize universities were allowed to read through the e-mails of associate professors. Anyway, he eventually pulled some strings for me, and had your division secretary look over your mail. Among other things, there was a letter from a Professor Georg Vlassak, who is in the history department here at the University of Prague. Haverkamp, in desperation, finally took the letter, opened it, and gave me Vlassak's telephone number. This man would like to meet with you. We're stuck here for most of the day tomorrow anyway. Of course, it's up to you."

"Okay, I'll call this Vlassak." I hesitate. "What about our personal relationship? I mean, with the manuscript? Am I still supposed to be covering for you? I saw you wink at me."

"Please keep covering for me until that four o'clock meeting tomorrow afternoon. After that, I'm on my own." She makes a quick left turn and drives down a ramp into the underground parking area connected to our hotel. "Let's get you a room; then you can call Dr. Vlassak, and later check some of your e-mails on my computer. I imagine you have a bunch."

"Everly, my billfold was stolen in that home and I don't have a cent of money."

"Don't worry, I'll take care of everything. In Germany, though, you'll need to come up with another passport." As we walk toward the hotel's front desk she continues, "I suppose I should give somebody at Mercedes a call concerning the damage to our car."

"Right, but then just order another Mercedes. You certainly have sufficient funds to cover such an expenditure." I laugh. "Of course, I'll need to repay you once we're back in America."

We end up with a room for me three doors down from Everly. I'm glad she didn't insist we share a room. She paid for my room in cash. She later tells me she has plenty of crowns, and she'll loan me as many as I wish. Later, on the third floor, I follow her into her room to check my e-mails on her computer. It is then I experience a shock! There are more than 80 of them, most from places in the United States, but others from Europe and around the world. The majority of the e-mails deal with the large manuscript I am supposed to be writing. I plan to read them later, and maybe Everly can also help me with some, if she has time.

Everly calls an airport company about a new rental, but finds that another Mercedes cannot be obtained from Germany until late tomorrow afternoon. I listen as she gives information about the damage on the present car, which I had rented a week ago in Bavaria, and hear her discuss the necessary obligation of making a police report within 24 hours. She then gives me the phone so I can call Professor Vlassak.

This has to be one of the easiest calls I ever made. A secretary, who I find speaks passable German, quickly connects me with Vlassak, who speaks English with somewhat of an accent. He wastes no time and suggests the two of us meet around ten-thirty at his office, in what was the history department at the University of Prague. He explains at the present time, the university is somewhat like Heidelberg in that both students and faculty are spread around the city. He, however, is still in the original structure and provides me with precise directions.

The plan is then to have lunch with an important member of the Czech legislature at an establishment called the Prague Cafe. When I ask about the subject at hand, he tells me without hesitation, *The Prague Manuscript*. I thank him and promise to meet him in his office at ten-thirty.

Everly has already opted for a walk through areas of the city center, to be followed by an outdoor lunch, but she refuses to leave the hotel until I write a long e-mail to Ruth. I had planned to do this anyway. Everly grabs a hotel magazine and lies on her bed, waiting for me to finish. I briefly explain to Ruth what happened to me, and how I finally escaped this morning with help from a member of the Prague police force. I naturally give her my room number, along with my phone number. I remind her that Everly has her Berlin number and say, if I don't hear from her sometime this evening, I will call her myself. After this, I typed the words practically everyone in a relationship would type, that I miss her, and love her more than ever.

Later, when Everly and I leave the hotel for our walk and outdoor lunch, she tells me she will not be going with me to meet Professor Vlassak tomorrow morning, but will instead go through all of our e-mails, and then spend the rest of the morning over in the 'Little Section' visiting Wallenstein's Palace and Gardens. She reminds me again about our four o'clock meeting with the people at the Bohemian Central Press, and following that, our call about the status of our new vehicle.

"Now, Bob, as soon as we take a bit of a walk and get something to eat, we can come back here to the hotel, get in our present wounded car and drive to the airport. I want to glance at the Czech and English versions of our manuscript. I haven't looked in that locker for days. Considering the present state of your memory, I doubt you will recall that I left the French and German versions in Munich last week before we came here.

"Right now, though, keep a 'lookout' for a nice outdoor restaurant, one with a view. Another 15 minutes and I'll be fainting from hunger. But hey, let me start out giving this tour. You can correct me if I make a mistake." I notice she is grinning at me. I don't believe she intends to make any mistakes.

We stroll in the neighborhood of the great statue of King Wenceslaus on Horseback. "The patron saint of the Czechs," she says. "He's sort of saint to the Germans, too. For them he is Wenzel. The English-speaking world, of course, knows him as 'Good King Wenceslaus' from the Christmas carol."

"Right. Lived sometime before the year 1,000 and was killed by his very own brother. Typical. The Germans and Czechs have also been killing each other for hundreds of years. And yet, few nations of people are more alike. Even now you could strip down a thousand Germans and a thousand Czechs, mix 'em all up, and I will bet you a million bucks no one could tell one from another."

"Leave it to the professor to get down to the naked truth." She smiles. "But you know, Bob, I think the problem was different languages and somewhat different cultures."

"No doubt. But considering all that happened over the centuries, maybe they should have left the guns at home."

"Or the Germans could have brought in even more guns," I think I hear her mutter, though perhaps I misunderstood.

The huge open oblong part of the city where we now walk is filled with people from almost every European nation, and other nations as well. We hear Czech, English, German, Italian, French, Spanish, Russian and all manner of other Slavic languages, each one dissolving into the other as we walk. No one pays us the slightest bit of attention. Naturally not. We look exactly the same as 98 percent of them. Though Everly may be hungry, otherwise she seems totally relaxed. I, however, am not relaxed at all. Every panel truck, every faraway helicopter, even a speeding motor bike, unnerves me. And my memory is still shaky. I have only the vaguest overview of her manuscript, and remember even less about my hour-by-hour activities leading up to the time I was abducted.

Suddenly I stop short! Everly has disappeared. God, we were just now walking along together. How can this be? I look in every direction but she is gone. I am surrounded by strangers, literally frozen here in space as though again under the influence of some drug. But then I hear her voice.

"Bob, Bob, why are you stopping?" Lord, she is only a few yards ahead of me. I quickly move forward to catch up. She slowly begins shaking her head. "Bob, you know you seem to be limping just a little. Were you injured in that home?"

"Not to worry, Everly. It must have happened last night when I tried to escape. But I'm not doing badly considering the drugs I still have in me." She nods uncertainly and we continue on our way.

"So, what do we have here?" she asks. "Your third visit to Prague?"

"Yes, and because you are with me, I want this visit to be special. We want to see as many things as we can." I smile. "Just as your father and the university administration suggested."

She shrugs. As we continue strolling along she points out the great Church of our Lady before Týn, with its gothic spires, certainly one of Prague's most famous landmarks, and then later, we come upon the large Jan Hus monument in the old town square.

"Now old Hus was an interesting and tragic figure," she says. "Preached his fiery sermons in the Bethlehem Chapel in Prague. Hope I'm not giving you questionable information, but I think Hus said: 'I read my bible in German, but I fight in the language of the Czechs'! The German emperor Sigismund offered Hus safe passage to the city of Constance, where Sigismund looked the other way and allowed old Hus to eventually be burned at the stake! Not too honest, but I guess Hus was becoming too much trouble to have around." I nod in agreement.

I gaze at the architecture of this place and remember its history. Everly has already stopped and is carefully examining the large Hus monument. Practically everyone pauses here for at least a few moments. But suddenly I am laughing. "Everly, I was just wondering if perhaps Novotny might have placed a microphone in that communion cup Hus is holding there. Keeping tabs on us."

She nods. "From what I already know about Novotny, if he thought it would help him get hold of our research, he would put three mikes in that cup!"

"He seems to be a decent person."

"One of the nicest police officers I have ever met."

"He is Czech."

"I know that, Bob. Look, I spent an entire week alone here in Prague and had not the slightest problem with anyone. One has to keep everything in perspective. Ruth told me in one of our phone conversations that she insisted once to you, 'it only takes about one-half of one percent of the people of any society to wreck havoc on a grand scale'. The people who kept you prisoner in that home were a part of that small minority." She eyes me sharply. "But what's your plan regarding Novotny? Plan to soften my resolve? Let me tell you something. If the people here have a choice between staring into my piercing green eyes, or going up against a line of panzers, I assure you they will choose the latter."

"Okay, Everly, whatever you say. I guess I just get overly concerned occasionally. You haven't yet told me about the exact nature of your plans for the future."

"Don't worry so much. I may never tell you about my plans. Hey!" she calls out suddenly. "Up ahead there on the right! An outdoor restaurant with free tables. We can even see the Moldau River and the castle from there."

"The Czech name for that river is the Vltava," I say, as we approach our table with the view.

"Bet you for hundreds of years lots of important people called it, Die Moldau. I think I even remember a musical composition by that name."

"Right. Friedrich Smetana. A marvelous piece of program music describing the river. But he might possibly have called it the Vltava, too occasionally. Sorry." I smile at her.

"Bob, please stop lording it over me! Now get me some Czech beer. Pronto!"

"Okay, okay. Czech beer it is." I wave for a waiter. "Now let's order some food, then hopefully you can lay some more history on me." Everly orders a hefty sandwich to go with her beer. I also have Czech beer, accompanied by a large salad.

She looks across the river toward the castle. "One of these days I'm going to visit that place," she remarks. "I've always wanted to." She shades her eyes in order to have a clearer view. "Up there is the exact spot the Thirty Years War began. Did you know that?"

I grin at her. "I vaguely seem to recall something about it, but I'm certainly ready to learn more."

"Okay, good. Now it's rather early in the 17th century, and quite a few members of the Czech nobility are considering revolting against the Holy Roman Empire. The Austrian Hapsburgs were controlling the empire out of Vienna at the time, and I guess they thought they had better crack down on the Czechs before they get completely out of control. They sent a couple of representatives to Prague to let the folks here know who was really the boss in this part of Europe. Well, the Czechs decided to show those German-speaking Austrians a thing or two so, after a mock trial, they heaved the two Austrians right out of a high window in the castle up there. They landed in a dung heap so neither of them died. Such was the ignoble beginning of one of the most devastating wars in European history. The Austrians soon got their revenge, though, when they clobbered the Czech and German armies at a place called White Mountain, actually not far from here. Of course, we've already discussed this, back at the university."

"Right," I say, "and on the way back to the hotel I will point out the 27 horizontal crosses on the walkway there, marking the deaths of the Czech and German leaders who were executed by the Austrian Hapsburgs some months after White Mountain. Anyone can stroll right over these crosses, and thousands do every day."

"This is insane," Everly says, laughing. "You remember this history from the 17th century, but you don't remember the fall of the Soviet Union which took place around 1990."

"Is that what happened?" I say, smiling a little. But because of what Everly said a couple of minutes ago, I now realize what Novotny had meant earlier when he said, 'the Czechs always throw their best people out the window'. "Hey, Everly," I continue. "Do you remember the 'fun title page' you wrote back in January as the first page of your now famous manuscript?"

"Sure. It said *The Prague Manuscript: Unruly Czechs run wild!* And then you said 'Great, now we need only about seven or eight hundred pages of truth to back this up'. At the time you didn't know I had already completed the entire manuscript." She picks up her sandwich and polishes it off in a flash. I glance at her plate, not quite believing she has already finished eating. I continue nibbling on the remainder of my salad for awhile.

"Think we're finally finished with Novotny?" she asks finally.

"Well, I think he's probably given up on us. Of course, one never knows. Anyway, I'm glad you aren't planning to bring the manuscript back to your hotel room."

She shrugs. "It wouldn't have worked in any case. My room safe would never have been large enough to hold it." She stares at my salad. "Come on, Bob. Finish it off. I want to get out of here!"

I shrug, leisurely take the last few bites of the salad, gently place my fork next to the plate on the table, lift my beer stein in a silent toast to Everly, slyly wink at her, and then take my last swig of amber ale. She tosses enough crowns on the table to cover our meal, and we leave the restaurant.

On the way back to our hotel we stroll over the 27 horizontal crosses and, although Everly is interested, she had never heard of any of the protestant leaders who were put to death here. Of course, she had known Frederick, the Winter King, the principal protestant leader, escaped Prague after the Battle of White Mountain and raced back toward the north.

Within ten minutes we drove out onto the street from our underground garage. It will not take long to reach the airport. During our brief trip I constantly adjusted my right side mirror, trying to check on the cars behind us. And yes, I soon notice a large, powerful BMW following us. It is at that instant I fully understand the smashed-in right side of the Mercedes and the red paint. They had marked us, and now someone is following right on our tail! They must have been parked on the street, just outside our hotel. Everly has already noticed the two men inside the car in her own mirror, and tells me they look exactly like the two who had been following her that first evening when she drove to the airport to hide the manuscript. "I'm sure they were looking for you that night, Bob. They seemed to have no real interest in me."

Once near the main terminal building, Everly puts the car into the only parking spot available that one can see, and races inside to check on the manuscript. The men in the BMW go on past, but only about 30 feet or so. There are no other places to legally park, and if the men drive on farther they are perhaps afraid they will lose track of us altogether. They aren't willing to risk this; instead, they abandon their car, even though it is completely blocking one lane of traffic, and come after me on foot. Both of them! Their approach, however, is interrupted by a young police officer who points sternly back toward their own car. He wants it moved immediately. The men argue, but this only makes the young officer angrier. He now asks for the driver's identification. His right hand is resting on his weapon. The driver of the BMW has to produce his papers, although both he and his partner appear almost frantic. At that instant Everly hurriedly exits the terminal building. I am astonished because she appears to be carrying a version of the 700 plus pages certain people would just love to steal. The boxes are in a large plastic sack.

"Everly, drive slowly past that scene up ahead," I tell her when she is behind the wheel again. "The two men in your BMW have been stopped by the police. Once you're by them, go the speed limit, but no faster. Thank God for that officer. The two men were coming at me on foot. They seem desperate for some reason."

"Yeah, because of us!" She backs out of our parking space and we move slowly ahead. Later we drive toward the airport exit at the maximum allowable speed. I keep glancing around toward the parked BMW, now far behind us. Finally I see the two men are being allowed to return to their car. But then, the mistake! The driver floors their vehicle in an attempt to overtake us, causing it to slide sideways out of control. The young officer is immediately on his phone. So, I think, the great Prague car chase will soon be under way! I am convinced we are now in mortal danger!

"Take off, Everly! They're coming after us. Anything the traffic will allow!" The problem is their car might possibly prove to be just as fast as ours and, as I watch, it does seem they are even gaining little by little. The two men inside are waving frantically for us to pull over. The police, of course, are on our side, at least for the moment; in fact, I can already hear the 'heehaw, heehaw' sounds of them coming, and from more than one direction. I have often heard people remark, 'it all seemed to happen in slow motion'. This was just the opposite. 'Definitely fast motion'.

By the time we are two blocks away from the airport, the BMW is practically right up against our back bumper. It is at that instant that a third vehicle, a gray Audi, roars down a ramp toward us, coming from the right and, as the back window behind the driver lowers, and an automatic weapon appears, I scream for Everly to cut left into the oncoming traffic, regardless of the danger of crashing! The men in the Audi, having spotted us because of our crumpled blood-red right side, have already shot out our back window. It is then, however, we are more or less saved by the very men we had previously feared— the two individuals in the large black BMW. They had been glued to us for many seconds and, when Everly made her desperate left turn into the traffic, they followed us, giving us a lot of protection. There is disorder in the streets! At least 20 other drivers are blasting on their horns and slamming on brakes, trying to avoid an accident.

It is a brief encounter. The police soon stop all traffic, except for the gray Audi which has already raced away toward the city center. A single police vehicle has followed it, though I suspect this pursuit is futile. Our car has come to a complete stop a scant three feet ahead of the BMW. By now seven police officers have gathered around, ordering us from our cars and inspecting the damage on the two vehicles. We would later learn a total of 38 bullets had struck our cars. The passenger in the BMW has a flesh wound and is now receiving first aid. Two officers stand with Everly and myself on the right side of the Mercedes, staring at the previous massive damage. One of the officers speaks passable English.

"At first I thought it was an act of vandalism," I tell him. "I realize now they had been marking us."

"In order to identify us," Everly puts in, "and then kill us!"

"Any idea why?" the officer asks quietly.

"No idea," I answer quickly. "We're just here researching a book dealing with Czech history." I nod back toward the two men standing in front of the BMW. "What's with those two? Their vehicle was shot up worse than ours."

"They are Israelis. That is about all I know. Now listen carefully to these instructions."

He turns to Everly now since she had been driving. "You will follow the police cruiser in front of you to the main police station in the city center. Another cruiser will follow you, which will be followed by the BMW, and still another cruiser. We have already decided the two of you were the principal targets here. And so, let us get this parade started."

"Amazing," Everly says a few seconds later as we slowly follow the lead cruiser.

I am already looking over some of the 700 pages I am holding on my lap. I grin at the title page, which I see is in English. After checking through several pages from both boxes I stop and relax. I am quite certain I understand what we have here. I smile. If Novotny is in this particular police station, I know he will grab for these pages immediately. I return the two boxes to the large plastic sack.

Sitting in the Central Police Station in the front row on Everly's left, I am amazed to see so many people in attendance. I am glad to see Novotny is present, though he appears not to be in charge. A very tall, thin, bald man stands on the small stage, accompanied by a heavyset seated woman on his left, whom I'm guessing is a translator. Novotny is also on the stage, but is seated somewhat behind the standing gentleman, off to his right. Novotny's gaze is focused almost exclusively on Everly, who is holding the sack containing the two manuscript boxes on her lap.

Directly behind me in the second row are the two Israelis, and far behind them, in the last row actually, are four people I have already met—the middle-aged man and woman from the home, and the two strange soldiers with whom I have battled more than once. Occupying almost the exact right center of the room are four of the police officers who were present at the end of the car chase, including the man who speaks English. Except for the small stage in front, the entire setting is reminiscent of an American grade school classroom. The meeting begins with the tall man introducing Novotny as his second in command and the seated lady, whom I have correctly assumed is a translator. She is already hard at work, translating everything being spoken into Czech. The tall individual, whom I can only think is the chief of police, is Boris Krecheck, and he tells us he will make a few remarks. Although he has a strong accent, his English is still easily understood.

"We are deeply troubled by what has happened here this afternoon," he begins. "Although we do not yet have the perpetrators in custody, we do have a license plate number, and therefore it should only be a matter of time before the criminals are apprehended." The tall man now turns his eyes downward toward Everly and myself, while the translator takes down his previous remarks on her computer.

"Though I have not yet been thoroughly briefed concerning this entire matter, those more knowledgeable of the case than myself, seem convinced it may hinge on a certain manuscript which has been researched and written by Dr. Robert Westbrook, assisted by Ms. Everly Somerset, both seated here in the front row." His eyes bore into mine now. "There is also the curious fact that Dr. Westbrook evidently decided, for some unknown reason, to spend six days in one of our homes for senior citizens here in Prague, and only left this home earlier this morning."

"What the hell!" Everly says loudly. "Just what is that supposed to mean?"

"Easy, Ms. Somerset." The tall man forces a smile now. "I would hate to have a girl as beautiful as yourself residing in one of our old folks homes." His smile begins to fade immediately.

I nudge Everly softly to keep her quiet, because I am already beginning to realize, this man is not our friend. There is a slight hesitation as he turns back toward Novotny.

"Because Mr. Novotny, my second in command, has a somewhat broader understanding of this case, I should like for him to make a few remarks at this time. He will also interview each person individually at a later hour."

Novotny stands, nods toward his boss, and then gazes around the room. He mentions the man and woman in the extreme back of the room, as well as the two soldiers sitting next to them, the four police officers from our chase, and finally the two Israelis. It turns out the middle-aged man and woman really are in charge of the home in which I had been kept, but Novotny appears to have little interest in them. Instead, he turns his attention to the two Israelis.

"Please state your names and the reason you are attending our meeting this afternoon."

"I am Jonathan Goldfarb," the tall, older man states, "Israeli intelligence. We have been searching for Dr. Westbrook for several days now. We believe Dr. Westbrook, seated here in the front row, has received a large grant from an old Nazi war criminal to help complete and then publish a work known as *The Prague Manuscript*."

"I am Erik Tannenbaum," the shorter, balding younger man states. "Also Israeli intelligence. We have reason to believe Dr. Westbrook's donor was a German soldier during the Second World War, and possibly a prison guard during the last months of that war. He could have been here in this country, perhaps in the city of Brno. Jews imprisoned here in the former Czechoslovakia were often sent on by train to places in Poland like Auschwitz." Although the two Israelis seem tough enough to have fought with the Spartans at Thermopylae, they both speak rather quietly and appear totally at ease.

Novotny eyes the two men carefully. He reaches up and scratches the right side of his neck, causing his little pistol to peep out from his left jacket pocket. "Please identify the German soldier and tell us here and now the amount of his donation."

"His name is Wilhelm Gertner," Goldfarb says, "and the exact amount of his donation was $1,900,000."

Everly is smiling pleasantly. I grin over at her and then look up at Novotny again. "Sure, I received a grant from an old German officer. The amount will go a long way in helping us promote our large manuscript." I glance over my shoulder at the two Israelis. "Nice work, men. I congratulate you." I notice Novotny seems to have more interest in the large package Everly is holding than in the discussion of any old war criminal. He turns back toward his boss again and they have a short discussion in Czech.

"Gentlemen," Novotny finally continues. "This is all very interesting but we have other matters to discuss here, including the attack on your two automobiles. Mr. Tannenbaum, how is your wound coming along? Will you need hospital care?" Tannenbaum slowly shakes his head. Novotny gazes around the room again. "I believe it is going to be necessary to limit our discussion of this subject to five additional minutes. Any more questions?"

"Where is the old soldier now?" Goldfarb asks me.

"If you are looking for a name, an address, or a phone number, I don't have a thing for you."

"Then how did the money get into your bank?" Tannenbaum asks pointedly.

I smile, I think rather slyly. "It's in a safety deposit box in Denver, Colorado. I just walked into my bank one afternoon carrying a small suitcase. Of course, I had met personally with my donor earlier, actually at his mansion in Lake Forest, Illinois. He had called me and given me the address. But, because I did not ever expect to see him again, I later tossed the paper with the street and number away." (This is a lie, as Everly and I needed the address in order to send the old soldier his copy of the manuscript. The address is now in a drawer in my university office.)

"What do you remember about this Colonel Gertner?" asks Goldfarb.

"He told me he was in the Caucasus, or near the Caucasus. This was where, as he said, 'my legs were shot out from under me'. His unit was trying to break through to the oil. He is perhaps 90 years old, and needs two crutches to get around. He has a young man of about 30 staying with him, who is also German. The older gentleman said he was given a desk job during the remainder of the war, though also somewhere in the East. His English is perfect, his demeanor almost aristocratic. I would guess he was an officer in the German Wehrmacht. I know nothing about him being a prison guard. His young wife died in the fire bombing of Dresden. They had no children. He seemed to have contempt for Hitler and mentioned, in his opinion, the killing of the Jews and the Dresden bombings, were the two greatest outrages of the central European war."

"What else did the two of you discuss?" Tannenbaum asks.

"The rest of our meeting dealt with *The Prague Manuscript*. He asked a few pertinent questions. He also told me, getting a tax-deduction for his donation through my university would be worthless, as his physicians have told him he is dying. They are giving him at most six months." I take a deep breath. "Frankly, this man did not seem like a war criminal."

"Few of them do," Goldfarb remarks. "And now, the final question: how can you help us find this elderly German?"

"No problem. I can drive you there, providing Mr. Novotny here ever allows me to leave the Czech Republic. I'm certain I can find the large mansion again."

"We've already been to the mansion," Tannenbaum says abruptly. "The old soldier was not there. There is a 'for sale' sign on the lawn."

"Perhaps he passed on," I say. "Remember, he admitted to me he was quite ill."

"Okay," Novotny breaks in. "Let's change the subject." The translator appears to be keeping up with the conversation. "Ms. Somerset, who do you think is trying to kill Dr. Westbrook and yourself?"

"Someone who desperately fears our manuscript. You see, they have to kill us here in the Czech Republic. I am holding two boxes containing the English version of our manuscript here on my lap. What if you or your superior, Mr. Krecheck, confiscated these boxes? It would mean nothing. After returning to Denver we would simply take one of our other copies, publish it, and then advertise it worldwide, using Mr. Gertner's large donation to help defray costs. So again, either we are killed, or we publish. In my opinion, considering what happened less than an hour ago, I submit, either you need to give us armed guards, or grant us safe passage to the German or Austrian border. I really wonder if you dare keep us here."

"Anything else?" Novotny asks her.

"Yes. A few days ago when I drove to the airport with this very manuscript," she touches the package she is holding, "Mr. Goldfarb and Mr. Tannenbaum followed me in their own car. I expect they were looking for Dr. Westbrook. Then, this morning, while at the old folk's home, someone smashed our car on the right side in three places, using red paint to help others identify it. The men in the Audi zeroed in on this damage before they began firing."

Novotny turns back to the Israelis again. "What do the two of you know about this manuscript? Please be blunt if need be."

"The manuscript is approximately 700 pages in length," Goldfarb answers. "It deals with the murders of thousands of mainly innocent Germans and Hungarians after the Second World War ended. However, we're also certain it deals with crimes against Czechs and Jews during the war. You simply cannot imagine how interested we are in seeing this manuscript first hand."

"All exaggeration!" Krecheck cries out. "This is all propaganda from Jews, and Sudeten Germans living in Bavaria or Austria. If this is what this young girl here is clutching so carefully, well, I can assure you I will see the pages torched before the day is out!" He angrily slams his left fist into his open right hand!

Novotny hesitates for a couple of seconds, then he smiles down at Everly. "And so, what are you clutching, Ms. Everly? Anything interesting?"

Everly stands and presents Novotny with the boxes. "*The Prague Manuscript,*" she says softly. She sits down again.

"One last question," Novotny asks the Israelis. "What do you know about a man by the name of Kriegsbaum?"

Goldfarb and Tannenbaum stare at each other. Within seconds they are both shaking their heads.

"Nothing?"

"Never heard of him," Goldfarb answers. "The name must mean 'tree of war', or some such thing."

Novotny, who has been holding both boxes under his left arm, now turns and hands one of them to Krecheck. "And so, shall we?" he suggests.

"Damned right! Just let me at this monstrosity!"

Novotny opens the lid of his full box. The first page must have jumped out at him and punched him in the face. It actually causes him to blink. Still, he reads it aloud. *"The Prague Manuscript: Unruly Czechs run Wild!* What the hell!" He claws at the succeeding pages. There is nothing. Krecheck hurriedly grabs at the first pages of his box. Here there is not even a title page.

"What the fuck is this?" he screams. The translator continues to pound on her computer. There are hundreds and hundreds of blank pages. This is all there is.

I slowly rise to my feet and meet Novotny's eyes. I have decided to call him Michael now. "Michael, you can't blame Everly for this. I had told her, were I ever to disappear here in Prague, she was to take the two boxes and hide them. These were the only two boxes left in my hotel room after she realized I was gone. I doubt Everly ever opened the boxes and looked inside."

"I didn't," she says, shaking her head.

"You know, Michael, you once asked me if I had mailed the 700 pages to anyone else. My answer was, 'I do not know', because I really couldn't remember earlier this morning. What a nice feeling it was, though, when shortly after noon I became aware that my memory was slowly beginning to return. I then realized that, some hours before those men abducted me a week ago, I had indeed sent the manuscript airmail to friends in America. This was the true manuscript. It's title page read, *'The Prague Manuscript: Czech Crimes Against German and Hungarian Civilians in Czechoslovakia, 1945-46'.* The only thing Everly took away that night was a lot of blank paper."

Both Novotny and Krecheck have lost it now! They grab handful after handful of the empty pages, throwing them high in the air until both boxes are empty. The pages float to the floor like large, flat snowflakes. Krecheck glares at Everly and myself. "I'm going to hold the two of you!" he yells angrily. "The charge? Subterfuge, yes, subterfuge!" He is pointing now toward the weird looking young soldiers in the last row. "Get the hell on this! Take this crap down the hall to my office. I'll use it for scratch paper." The soldiers have not moved. Perhaps they have not understood Krecheck's English. He springs from the stage and, halfway back to the men, throws the box he still has in his hand at their heads, now cursing in Czech. The two soldiers both quickly jump to their feet and rush forward to take care of the mess.

I have turned to watch this action, but I immediately focus on something even more dangerous and more sinister. Just like Jack Ruby, who shot Oswald right under their noses, I am thinking. The police chief was acquainted with the man and woman from the home, and so he had allowed them into the station without making them go through a weapon's check. I see the woman open her large purse and bring out two pistols. She hands one to the man on her left. All the while the two soldiers are cleaning up the thousand pieces of paper. Neither of them realize what is happening behind them. I believe the first bullet must have flown by my right shoulder and then struck Novotny, who is still standing on the stage, in the left thigh. By now both the man and woman are firing. Everly and I are down on the floor taking cover. Novotny is in a prone position on the stage and has his own small pistol out, preparing to shoot. Krecheck is standing down on the left, seemingly in shock. The two Israelis have gone to the floor like Everly and myself, a row behind us. By now Novotny is firing. From underneath the chairs I see the man in the last row is down. Either Novotny is lucky, or he is one hell of a shot! The woman's pistol is either empty by now, or has jammed. Two of the police officers, who had been sitting in the right center of the room, have now wrestled her down, and within seconds she is in handcuffs. Her partner appears to be dead.

Krecheck is still standing there like a zombie. I wonder if he hasn't already forgotten about arresting us. Everly and I stay with Novotny until the ambulance arrives, along with the Israelis and the last two policemen from our car chase. Novotny is grinning at us, putting pressure on his thigh, but I gather he feels the wound is unimportant. He tells us he will call Krecheck later and calm him down.

"You are getting to be my hero," I say. "What a great shot!"

He suddenly turns serious. "Don't ever think those bullets were meant for me, my friend. You and Ms. Everly had better do some serious talking soon, consider life in the near term." He nods to the Israelis and the two policemen. When the medics finally come and roll him away, he is already smiling again.

Everly and I motion to the Israelis to follow us and the four of us leave the police station at once, not even bothering to glance in Krecheck's direction. I don't see him anyway. I think he may have gone along with Novotny in the ambulance. We visit a nearby cafe and order coffee. I tell the Israelis about my meeting at the University of Prague with Professor Vlassak tomorrow morning at ten-thirty. I invite them to come with me. After glancing at each other for a couple of seconds, they agree to accompany me. "We'll have lunch later with an important member of the Czech parliament," I say. I give them careful directions to Vlassak's office.

After a few seconds, Goldfarb meets my eyes. "There is, of course, the question of the large donation."

"Herr Gertner made his money in the United States," I put in. "You can't touch it. Of course, he could have served in another army for awhile before immigrating." I smile.

Everly is shaking her head in disgust. "For God's sakes, the old man is almost 90 years old! I'm getting a little sick of seeing old soldiers harassed, and I don't give a damn which army they fought for! And just how did you get any of this information?"

"We've been trying to find Herr Gertner for many months," Tannenbaum says softly. "Our big break came a few days ago when we visited the large mansion in Lake Forest, and immediately afterward discovered a young man named David getting ready to board a plane to South America." Tannenbaum is smiling now. "Our friend, Gertner had boarded another plane, just the day before. Destination, Prague! That old man is 86 and, as you Americans sometimes say, 'fit as a fiddle'! The two crutches were a mere prop for your benefit,

Dr. Westbrook. He's headed for the city of Brno, the exact location of his last service in the German army. Want to accompany us there? You see, we need someone to identify him. We don't have a recent photograph. By the way, have you ever been to Brno? Do you know Moravia at all?"

I nod, but I give Tannenbaum no encouragement. "How do you know he is really a war criminal? Perhaps he was a mere army administrator in Brno. Remember, he told me he was fighting in the East until almost the end of the war."

"Possible," Goldfarb interjects. "We're still looking into that aspect. We leave for Brno early tomorrow evening. Why don't you join us?"

"Not a chance. Tell you what, you guys locate the old soldier, cart him back here, and I promise I'll identify him. But he did not give me a name. Perhaps it's Gertner, as the two of you believe."

Everly and I are ready to leave the cafe. We all shake hands and I remind the two Israelis to join me tomorrow at ten-thirty. I tell them I'm certain it will be an interesting meeting.

Later, Everly tells me she is glad she's decided not to attend the meeting. "No way in hell!" she continues. "I'm beginning to think I should never have given you Vlassak's name. God knows what's going to happen to you tomorrow."

"Why are you suddenly so worried? Is it because the Israelis are attending the meeting?"

"I'm not really sure. Maybe it's nothing."

"It's probably just nerves, Everly." I glance over at her. "Now, another subject. Remind me. Did you say you left half the manuscript in Munich?"

"Good God, Bob! You must still be full of drugs! We've already discussed this. Anyway, half is in Munich, and the English and Czech versions are still in a big locker at the airport. I've always had extra boxes of blank paper. I just put my silly title page at the front of one of them and, well, you know the rest. Because the Israelis were chasing us in their car, I certainly wasn't going to leave the terminal with the real thing. For all I knew, we were about to be robbed!" She shakes her head in frustration. "But, Bob, I'm worried about our situation here. Neither of us advertised our trip to Europe. No one here has read a word of *The Prague Manuscript*. So, I ask myself, why the desperate attempts on our lives? It's like we're being attacked by insane phantoms."

"I've been asking myself the same questions. I can only think other newspapers picked up on that Chicago article, or maybe people from Germany or Austria have been sending information about me to Prague. Several small newspapers published articles about me five years ago when my documentary film was coming out."

"And, of course, hundreds of copies were sold at the time. Let's not forget that. Actually, those former sales might possibly be the source of our problem. Could someone have translated your DVD into Czech?"

I shrug. "If they have, I've never heard of it." From where we are walking I can see the Jan Hus monument in the distance again. We had walked by it going in the other direction less than two hours before. I suddenly take her arm. "Everly, I would really like to visit Novotny in the hospital. Do you mind?"

"No, I want to see him, too." She smiles at me. "And I know right where they took him. That young policeman who spoke English told me. It's St. Luke's. We'll need a taxi, though. It's too far to walk."

"Right, and our car is crumpled and all shot up."

She laughs. "And impounded!"

When we locate Novotny's room in the hospital we find him eating a steak and drinking Czech beer. "A genuine tough guy!" I say, laughing. "Not even a guard on your door."

"You're the one they're trying to kill. Not me. By the way, they've located the gray Audi, parked along side a filling station. Not a terrorist in sight."

"Who do you think is doing all this?" Everly asks.

"Oh, some old communists, or new Czech right-wingers. Who knows." He glances over at me again. "You weren't even the first innocent person to be held in that home. When I finally get to be chief, I plan to put a stop to everything along these lines. You know, the two of you should take a walk around that corner up there." He is pointing. "You'll find a certain woman you both know."

"I would have thought she would be in jail," Everly says.

"I winged her. The left arm. I think the bullet must have bounced off a chair. But you'll find a guard at her door! Go and say hello. I know she'll appreciate it." He laughs. "Tell the guard I gave you permission to glance in."

Around the corner, Everly and I find a young policeman inside the room, sitting in a chair five feet or so away from the woman's bed. Perhaps he became tired of standing. The woman herself is strapped down. For me, it is a joyful sight. The young officer has already risen to his feet, wondering what is going on, what we are doing there.

"What goes around, comes around!" I call out to the woman. Then I give her the same phrase in German. Her face is filled with hatred. Both Everly and I are smiling.

The officer quickly walks up to us. I tell him Mr. Novotny gave us permission. Everly and I walk away then, not wanting to cause more commotion.

Back in Novotny's room, he asks us once again about our large manuscript. He takes another drink of beer while waiting for an answer.

"You will get your personal copy," Everly tells him. "We guarantee it. And don't worry, we'll still be around for awhile."

Novotny frowns. "I wouldn't if I were you. Go to Austria or Germany. Send the manuscript to me by mail." Everly and I look at each other, though not really surprised by his statement. For several seconds it is quiet in the room. It turns out, though, Everly has an important question for him.

"What happened back in 1945-46, Mr. Novotny? Sometimes as I read the history, I'm convinced certain of the Czech males must have gone insane for a few months. I would really appreciate your viewpoint on this."

"Well, I have my own ideas. Like the woman strapped down around the corner, with her Nazi-like mercenary soldiers, there were even more such people at the end of the big war. One must remember, we had been ruled by the Austrian Hapsburgs for approximately 400 years, and then again by the

Germans during the Second World War. Most of the Czech people resented this entire history. I believe many of the German citizens living in Czechoslovakia at the end of the war must have thought things would be about the same as they had been after the First World War. Maybe they would have to lay low for awhile, but that would be the extent of it." He looks at us both seriously. "But then the killing began. Places like Aussig."

"There was an explosion at a factory there," Everly interrupts. "The Czechs blamed German civilians, and because of this, they killed several hundred of them within 24 hours. Some were thrown off a bridge on the Elbe River."

Novotny looks at her curiously. "You have such a grasp of the details at your young age. I can scarcely believe it! Anyway, the killing began throughout the country as soon as the war ended. How many Germans died? I have no idea. The Sudeten Germans living in Bavaria speak of the fantastic number of 131,000. Frankly, this account seems absurd to me. But many were killed, and of all ages. Let us admit it.

"Did Czech farmers simply walk across the fields and murder their German neighbors? Hardly. The killers often came in flat bed trucks from Prague and other cities; many were probably drunk and, in almost every case, they were killing people they did not know. But the most horrible aspect of the killing was this: the young Czech men had missed the big war. They had not fought. But who was occupying their country during this war? Why, Germans, of course. And so, they had their own little war against German civilians later! And so, Ms. Everly, in a way some men really did go insane at that time.

"These are simply my ideas on the subject. I know you, Dr. Westbrook, have been wondering how I learned my American English. When I was very young, there were almost 30,000 Americans here in Prague. They earned their meager living by teaching American English. I learned my English from them." He gives us both a smile and offers his hand. We both take it warmly. As we leave his hospital room, I think I will always remember him as being one of the most decent human beings I have ever known.

"So, what's next on the agenda?" Everly asks as we leave the hospital. "Frankly, I'd like to stay together for awhile. I'm wound up as tight as a drum."

"Let's grab a cab and get back to our area of the city. Then we'll have a few drinks and talk. When I consider what happened to us just today, well, I still can't believe it! And we have plenty of time. There is no sense trying to call Ruth in Berlin for at least two hours."

She takes my hand as we walk toward the corner where cabs are available. "Ruth will understand," she tells me, giving me a squeeze.

"Don't worry about it. We're both emotional wrecks! What say we later go to a nice establishment and hang one on? Jesus, we deserve it." Everly sees a cab and flags it down, but she holds onto my hand all the way back to the 'Old Town' section.

Later, sitting in the middle section of an upscale bar and grill, nursing our drinks, I ask her about the Bohemian Central Press. "Your father bought them off, yet they've never even seen the manuscript. Are you sure it's really important to meet with those editors?"

"Of course, why not? A lot of money has changed hands. Let's see what they say. Do you doubt they'll publish the manuscript?"

"I have mixed feelings. You're occasionally quite rough on the Czechs. Some would say, over the top. And I have two other concerns. First of all, I agree with Novotny. He feels it would be better if we left the Czech Republic as soon as possible. Secondly, I wish you would remember how many decades have passed since the end of the Second World War. It is quite possible every last person who harmed members of your family has been dead for years."

"Maybe." She takes a hefty drink of scotch. "But this country has escaped almost unscathed for the criminal acts committed in the months after the war. I intend to make certain the world is made aware of those acts of terror!"

"Does your newly acquired wealth fit into these future plans?"

"Naturally. It fits perfectly."

"Why in the name of God don't we talk about these plans. I mean, everything. You must know how interested I am."

"Promise you won't try and stop me?"

I hesitate for a few seconds. "I'm not sure. How many people do you think are going to die?"

She smiles. "How many Sudeten Germans were killed here in 1945-46?"

I don't answer her. We both silently deal with our drinks. But this last statement bothered me, namely, her flippancy dealing with the number of deaths.

"I really need you to stick by me tonight," she says finally. "Today has been too much! It's a shame you have to be tied up emotionally with Ruth, especially at this time."

"But I love her," I say quietly. I watch as she drains the last of her scotch.

"I need another drink," she tells me, handing over her glass. She then goes into her purse and yanks out what appears to be twelve or fourteen hundred crowns and euros, and stuffs them into my hand.

I grin at her. "Okay, I'll take care of it." Glancing down at the money, I tell her I think it will be enough for tonight. I stand and walk to the bar. When I return with her drink, I notice she is drumming her fingers on the top surface of our small table. She immediately lifts the glass and takes another big drink of scotch.

"All right," she says softly, "I'll tell you about some of my plans. Our manuscript is to be published, of course, in English, German, French, and Czech. I know you are aware it has already been translated from the original English by people in New York. Following publication, full page ads will be taken out in newspapers in large cities in Europe and the United States. Many war time Czechs will be described as having been brutal killers, and it will be hammered home that they, and their families, should be held morally accountable for these actions. Furthermore, the present Czech government should strike one of the Benes decrees in order to allow modern day German citizens to return to their ancestral homeland to live as they wish. Finally, helicopters will drop millions of leaflets throughout the Czech Republic, repeating the same message in Czech that newspapers in the country have already printed." She looks at me seriously. "Okay, so far?"

"I don't suppose the leaflets will result in anyone's death. So, what's next?"

She lifts her glass and takes another drink. "Why, that's it. Don't you think it's enough?"

I take a sip of scotch myself. "That's not the end of it. Why are you afraid to tell me the whole story?"

"I'm not afraid. It's just fun to keep you in the dark. Let's change the subject. Talk about our manuscript. Who do you think is the most knowledgeable about the atrocities that occurred in this country during and after the war?"

"You are. You copied everything from my documentary film, *Brothers at War*, and then you piled on thousands of additional facts coming from that professor in Chicago. Without question, you are the most knowledgeable."

"Let's test it. What happened in Landskron?"

I look at her, shaking my head. "I'm certain you know the facts, but I still have an advantage. I can picture the place in my mind. You see, I've been there. The cemetery is on a flat place. It is well kept. The grave stones are practically all Czech. Some German. At the far end of the cemetery is a mass grave containing at least 40 innocent Germans who were murdered beginning May 17, 1945. Partisans arrived in the town in trucks and incited the locals to begin rounding up Germans, most of whom had been living in the area for as long as anyone could remember."

"I know most of that. So, what's new?"

"Ah, but I can still picture the town square. And, as I think back, I imagine the machine gun, and the table where the phony jurors were sitting. I envision a woman wearing some kind of uniform, who stands apart from the others. She is among the most vicious of the group. It is a mock trial, Everly, not unlike the trial you described yesterday at lunch, just before the Czechs threw the two Austrian diplomats from Vienna out a window in the castle. But, again, standing in the town square, looking up the gentle slope I see in the upper left corner, an extremely large basin filled with water. Czech men, wearing a strange assortment of uniforms, are holding the heads of German civilians under water until they drown. I turn my head only slightly to the right and I see other Germans being hanged. The one German man had just happened to come to town that day on some kind of errand. No matter. The Czechs grabbed him and hanged him, too! Some of the partisans standing around are wearing caps from Rommel's Africa Corps. They were always fond of them."

"What are you telling me? The entire scenario you described took place years and years before you were born."

"A couple of members of our historical group were children when this all happened. The father of one of the women with me had been hanged that day. After our filming was completed, we all entered an upscale restaurant there on the square where I had one of the best meals of my life. I remember observing the Czech people there in the dining area; so cultured, so controlled. One elderly gentleman came to our table and addressed us in German. He had seen us filming out in the square. We had a short, pleasant conversation. And then later, I asked myself: How had it happened the ancestors of these cultured people, blood relatives of Palacky, Smetana, Dvorak, Dubcheck, and Havel, could have committed all those monstrous acts? Of course, the world has been asking Germans the same question for decades."

For a few seconds neither of us speak. We are both dealing with our drinks. Everly continues to consume twice as much alcohol as myself. "I have never made love to an intoxicated woman," I say, teasing her a little. She glares at me; then she takes another big slug of scotch. Her eyes have become mere slits.

"Bruenn!" she says forcefully, slamming her fist down on the small table between us, bouncing our glasses around.

"Okay, Bruenn. Well, this is interesting. Sometimes, while being held in the home, I would have dreams so terrible I would wake up screaming. You know, mainly because of the drugs they were giving me. One of the most horrible dreams I had concerned the 'Bruenn Death March'."

"Something infinitely worse than anything that happened in Landskron. I suppose this description will need to go on nearly forever."

"Not if you don't want it to. Tell you what, why don't you discuss the 'Death March'? I'll just listen in. How many German civilians do you think died that day?"

"There are different estimates. I've heard 6,000. Others say 2,000."

"Which figure is in our manuscript?"

"2,000. I was conservative."

"How did it all come about?"

"You know damned well how it came about! Czech partisans and factory workers went from house to house rounding up the German population, the young, the old, the middle-aged, and herded them onto a road leading to the Austrian border. Most of the partisans wore something red, an armband, or perhaps a scarf. Many identified with the Soviet communists. Well, they would certainly regret having that attitude after awhile."

"How did they decide whom to shoot, or beat to death? And did they kill the kids, too?"

She hesitates and takes another drink. "I imagine they killed anyone who slowed them down. They wanted the Germans out of the country as quickly as possible."

"Half of the ditches must have eventually been full of bodies. That's the way I remember it from my dream." I take another small sip of scotch.

"I just can't imagine them killing the kids," Everly says, absently.

"Well, I'm glad you feel this way. Speaking of the young, though, I do believe I've read that some Czech teen-age males, when they saw an older German man or woman fall to the ground, unable to go further, well, they would rush forward and stomp on them for awhile."

"Jesus Christ!"

"Yes, you might say so. Many must have cried to a higher power for help that day. The 'Bruenn Death March' was a very bad scene indeed! Well, let's get on with it. We only have a few hundred other examples of murder and mayhem to examine here in what is now the Czech Republic."

"Oh, to hell with all this!" Everly says in exasperation. She stands and hands me her phone. "It's about time to call Ruth. You already have the number. I'm going up to the bar and get us a couple more drinks. You said you wanted to 'tie one on'."

"But let's move forward gently. Remember, we are still planning to order something to eat."

While dialing Berlin I watch Everly at the bar. I notice she has ordered a single scotch and water for herself. I'm sure she will take her time drinking it there, in order to give me more privacy while talking with Ruth. I am lucky. Ruth answers the phone immediately. I begin by telling her how wonderful it is to hear her voice again, but she interrupts at once, saying we need to discuss Everly's situation before talking about ourselves. Her attitude surprises me as she generally tends to be a rather calm, laid-back person, and I can't imagine what is so important we lack the time to even say hello to each other.

"I've spoken with Everly four times, Bob, and I don't like what I'm hearing. I understand the tragic history of her family, but this is no excuse for what she is planning. You simply can't leave her in that country. There's a bullet waiting for her there! As soon as the Czechs discover she's the one who wrote the big manuscript, they'll go after her. How fast can you get her across the border into Germany?"

"We have a four o'clock meeting tomorrow afternoon with a Prague publishing company. That's it, as far as I know. The question is, will she come with me?"

"You have to make her listen! Where is she right at the moment?"

"I can see her. She is sitting at the bar, giving us some privacy for our conversation."

"What kind of person is she? Fill me in as best you can."

"That will be easy. Everly is extremely bright, beautiful, and filthy rich! She is also stubborn. I may have to say something like, 'Ruth wants desperately to meet you'. That might work."

"Leave as soon as your meeting is over tomorrow afternoon. You know, you have to get out of there, too! God knows what kind of people have been watching you! Now, I'll be back in Munich by midday Saturday, that's day after tomorrow. And, Bob, I received your e-mail from earlier today. Am I to understand you were abducted and held in some kind of home for almost a week? And given drugs?"

"You don't know the half of it! But so much has happened, frankly I would rather tell you about it Saturday in person. But don't worry about me. I feel I'm safe for now. Everly, always ready to help, paid for my room in her hotel with cash. No one knows where I am, and surely practically no one knows what I look like. Now tomorrow morning I'm meeting with a professor of history at the University of Prague, and then having lunch with him and a member of the Czech government. I should also mention that two Israelis will be joining us as far as I know."

"Okay, now just one more thing before we change the subject to ourselves." I hear her take a deep breath. "You say Everly has money?"

"She claims she has a few billion. Her family has been into mining for decades."

"Then under no circumstances should you allow her to use any portion of this money to harm the Czech people. Practically every criminal from that war, on all sides, is already dead. What does she expect to accomplish?"

"I don't know. How much did she tell you? I already know about the publication in four languages, the huge ads in newspapers in large cities throughout the western world, and the millions of leaflets. What else is there?"

"None of that is horrible, though the idea of dropping all those leaflets seems silly to me. But her next move must be stopped! She plans to hire at least 100,000 protesters, mainly from Hungary and Slovakia, and start them raising hell in every city in the Czech Lands. The protesters will be highly paid, and will take their jobs seriously. The Czechs don't have enough prison space to house them all, not even if they utilized every damned old folks home in the country. Believe me, Bob, somebody will kill her! You can count on it. As least as distasteful, will be the fact that perhaps several innocent Czech citizens will also die. Everly is counting on her protesters blocking every city center in the country. She can't be allowed to go forward with this idiotic plan!"

I hesitate for a moment as I watch Everly, who is still at the bar, and whom I see is ordering still another drink. "How far should I go? I've already told you she's stubborn. I swear to God she sometimes acts like a 15-year-old kid."

"Get her to Munich. We'll both work on her. But let's be honest, it's you I'm most worried about right now. The crazies still believe you are the author of *The Prague Manuscript*." For several seconds neither of us speak. We both know where the conversation is heading now. Ruth continues. "Bob, do you remember our phone call when you said we had serious matters to discuss when I come to visit you in Colorado?"

"Yes, and you suggested we discuss those matters right then."

"Exactly. You see, I was hoping you would propose to me that night."

"I wondered about that. But then later you began considering taking that new position in Berlin, and I think we had an argument about it. Following that, my university unbelievably pressured me into chaperoning Everly on a trip to Europe, and. . .well, you know the rest."

"Chaperoning Everly?" Ruth laughs. "Now, let me bring you up-to-date regarding my life. First of all, I made a mistake in transferring to Berlin; in fact, I'm returning to my job in Munich in about two weeks."

"But I guess this means you've given up on the idea of visiting me in Colorado this spring."

"Not necessarily. But it would have to be later in June. Now I'll have three days with you and Everly in Munich. Then I have to return to Berlin to close up shop here. Tell me, have you ever considered taking a teaching position in Germany?"

"No, but I think I'll start considering this if it's important to you. There is the possibility of teaching in an international school, of course."

"I love you as much as ever, Bob. Don't ever doubt it. But I've been think-ing about a lot of things. We can talk about them day after tomorrow. Shouldn't you be waving Everly over? She's been sitting alone at the bar for a long time. I think I'm really going to like her. Please get her safely across the border!"

"I love you, Ruth. I'm counting the hours." But then I realize the connection is already broken. I wave to Everly to join me. I watch her as she walks toward me. "So, have you calmed down a little?" I ask, after she is seated again.

"Not completely. How's Ruth? Is she coming back to Munich eventually?"

"Yes, and she'll be there on Saturday, just as you said. But Monday she has to return to Berlin to sort of close up things there. I think she wants me to come and teach in Germany. My guess is she doesn't wish to move permanently to the United States, though she did say she might visit me in Colorado sometime in June."

"And your response?" I'm watching Everly carefully now and am astonished when I see her take still another hefty drink.

"Well, I hope she does visit me in Colorado." I smile at her.

"I don't mean that, you idiot! What about the other?"

"I haven't had time to consider it. I only learned of the situation about five minutes ago." I look at her seriously. "Everly, I want you to go with me to Munich to meet her."

"The two of you need to be alone. And I have things to do here."

"What things? Hell, let's turn in two versions of our manuscript tomorrow afternoon, one in Czech, one in English, and then come back and talk with the editors at the publishing company in a few days. I really wish you'd come with me to Munich, Everly."

"I'll think about it." I see her glancing toward a waitress. "Wonder if we could get something to eat. I'm beginning to feel strange."

"I can imagine. And I'll take care of it." I notice something is wrong, though, because I see her suddenly lie down in the booth, with her legs dangling out into the traffic. As I have no faith that Everly will be eating anything in this establishment any time soon, I order some items to go. In the meantime, I carefully slide her glass of scotch far to the right and hide it behind a menu. She certainly doesn't need any more alcohol. I haven't yet had even three drinks, and alcohol has never fazed me to the extent that it does certain other people. I continue to sip at my own drink, thinking over my life, and wondering what might possibly be facing me during the next several days.

I can just see the top of Everly's head and admit that, were she not with me now, drunk or not, I would already be somewhat depressed and lonely. However, my mind is mainly on Ruth. I am considering her comments, especially the idea of eventually teaching in Germany. I am not adverse to this plan. But, on another level, our conversation was shocking. The idea of Everly hiring 100,000 protesters to disrupt cities in the Czech Republic seems mindless and borderline criminal.

If I had my way, I would somehow persuade her to accompany me to Munich, and then Ruth and I could perhaps convince her to get on a plane bound for Denver. There is another reason I would be in favor of this plan. Everly is too damned beautiful to constantly have around! At that moment I see my waitress approaching, carefully avoiding Everly's dangling legs. She hands me a bag containing a couple of sandwiches and French fries.

But now, the question is: how can I move Everly? Not easily. It takes us more than half an hour to reach our hotel and, by the time we leave the elevator in the hotel and stagger toward her room, I am having to hold her up. As I take her card to open her door, I am concentrating with all my strength on Ruth, the girl I love. A good thing, too. Once inside the door, Everly throws her arms around my neck and begins kissing me hard on the mouth. After three or four seconds I gently push her away, thanking her for the sweet kiss.

She looks like a child at that moment. "If it was so sweet, why did you stop me?"

"Because of your condition perhaps. I generally prefer lively girls."

"I might could get lively," she says in a small voice.

"You might could get lively? Frankly, I doubt it. Not tonight." I lead her further into her room. Then I say all the practical things a decent man says under the circumstances, especially one who is in love with another woman: go to the bathroom, put on your pajamas, be careful not to fall, and remember, you are drunk. I turn down the covers on her bed and it is not long before she comes from the bathroom and sort of slithers under them.

"Watch that you don't get dizzy and fall out of bed," I say. I then point to the bag containing the food which I have placed on her bed stand. "Don't gulp it; just nibble."

"If you would stay by me, you could hold me and keep me from falling out of bed."

"You'll be okay. Good night, girl child." I turn away and go back to my own room.

I don't bother Everly in the morning; instead, I have a late breakfast alone, and then walk toward the university shortly after ten o'clock. I meet Erik Tannenbaum and Jonathan Goldfarb near Vlassak's office in the history department, just as we had planned, and almost immediately Professor Vlassak steps into the hallway to join us. I introduce the two Israelis and the professor seems happy they are with me. We follow him into his office.

Dr. Vlassak is a tall, good-looking Czech, who I gather is the equivalent of our head of a history department. He laughs and tells us he is amazed we have traveled so far to meet him. I notice the faces of both Erik and Jonathan remain somewhat rigid. Perhaps they suspect the name of the supposed old Nazi war criminal may soon enter the discussion. I imagine they want to be ready to join the conversation. Also, news of the attack on us yesterday afternoon will undoubtedly have already reached all areas of the news media. Still, I am not particularly worried about anything. Surely our meeting this morning had not been widely publicized. My goal is to attend these two meetings in civilized fashion, meet with people at the Bohemian Central Press this afternoon with Everly, and then return to Germany, hopefully with Everly sitting at my side.

Vlassak is asking a few questions now. "Dr. Westbrook, in your opinion, might *The Prague Manuscript* be of interest to law enforcement officials in either the United States or Europe?"

"I doubt it," I tell him. "As you may already know, our manuscript deals with the atrocities committed against Czech, Jewish, German, and Hungarian civilians during and after the Second World War. The people who committed these crimes are either deceased, or already so old I doubt anyone would bother prosecuting. We believe, however, we have dealt fairly with the history of all crimes committed between 1939 and 1946 in what is now the Czech Republic."

Vlassak speaks passable English, though with a heavy accent. "We hear your research is unbelievably thorough. Why have you been so meticulous if you don't intend to see any justice carried out?"

I laugh. "Just my nature, I guess. But I'll bet your own books and articles are also carefully written."

No one says anything for a few seconds. Finally, Jonathan Goldfarb joins the conversation. "Professor Vlassak, I know, as a citizen of Prague, you are well acquainted with the history of the Jewish people here. The placard over in the Jewish section brings that history to light. Tens of thousands of Jews were shipped away during the time of the Third Reich. None that I know of returned. This is the main reason my colleague and I are looking forward to receiving a copy of *The Prague Manuscript*. We already know it deals in part with the deportation of Jews from here into Poland during the war."

"I can certainly understand your interest in this large book," Vlassak answers him. "I want to see the manuscript myself, and as soon as possible. The history of the Jewish people here in central Europe in the 20th century was an abomination, and carried out by mass murderers." He turns his attention to me again. "Dr. Westbrook, I would greatly appreciate it if the four of us could take a few minutes to examine both the history of our small country and it's future. We are a tiny landlocked nation, not at all rich, and we cannot sustain much economic upheaval. Frankly, certain aspects of your research worry me." He is slowly shaking his head. "We are surrounded by nearly one hundred million Germans on three sides. A bit unnerving."

"You're counting the Austrians," I say, laughing.

"Well, German speaking."

"Let's be honest. Germany is not your enemy. You may be reliant on the Germans economically more than you would like, but there will be no further military action against the Czech Republic any time in the future. Your country is in both NATO and the European Union. Any future attack by Germany is unthinkable."

"What about the manuscript itself? How much is my country to be hammered? Most people here don't want to know about any atrocities. They don't want to learn about any properties stolen from German people in the Sudetenland after the war. They want to forget it all!"

I nod in understanding, though preparing to lie once again. "As I have told others before, my assistant and I have been entirely neutral about what happened here in the middle of the last century. While our huge volume presents thousands of facts, and may even cause some to adjust their view of   history slightly, I don't believe the publication will weaken this nation to any substantial degree. It's only a book, after all, and I doubt there are 20 people in Prague right now who have ever heard of our research."

Vlassak smiles at me then and backs away from the table. Erik and Jonathan seem even more attentive now. I think perhaps they have an inkling about what is coming. I am completely in the dark. Vlassak leans forward again and hands me a section of today's main Prague newspaper, which he has taken from a small table behind him. The first thing I notice is my photograph, and then my name in large print at the top of the section of the paper he has given me. I can't read the article, of course, and I look to Vlassak for clarification. I assume the entire page under my name deals with our large manuscript.

"It is very tough," Vlassak says. "In fact, I would say its tone is almost threatening. At one point it is suggested your motive is to stir up the Sudeten Germans in Bavaria again, and bring them, as the article says, 'to the frenzy of revenge'. The $2,000,000 grant is also discussed in detail, and for the Czech people, this is an immense amount of money. It is easy for someone here to imagine, with these kinds of funds, you will be able to spread your propaganda around the world. The large article ends with the statement: 'This mad professor is obviously attempting to weaken the Czech Republic'!"

"I can read Czech," Erik says abruptly. "Might I see the paper?" Jonathan is looking on from the side, presumably at the large photograph of myself. Vlassak and I wait for several seconds until Erik finishes reading.

I smile and glance over at Vlassak. "Well, now I know how you learned so much about my manuscript. People here seem to have been doing quite a lot of writing."

"Yes. There were other smaller articles during the past month. It's probable that a significant percentage of the Czech population has at least heard of you." He looks at the three of us seriously now. "What I'm still in the dark about is who contacted the paper regarding this article. It seems like it might be the work of Petroevski, or perhaps Drtina."

"We were both interviewed by the paper," Jonathan admits, "right after the two attacks on Dr. Westbrook's life yesterday. Of course, we had also wanted to get out the word on Herr Gertner." He turns quickly to Professor Vlassak again. "I'm wondering about the other individuals you just mentioned: Petroevski and Drtina. I don't believe I've ever heard of them."

"They are extreme right-wing politicians. To me, they are practically Czech Nazis!" Vlassak glances at me again. "How can I get a copy of your large manuscript?"

"I will personally send you a copy. With pleasure. Your copy will actually be in the Czech language."

He nods in appreciation, and then looks toward the Israelis again. "And so, according to today's paper, the two of you are chasing a Nazi war criminal. He must be a very old man."

"Old, but still quite lively actually," Eric says. "We believe he is in Brno at the present time. We plan to travel there later this afternoon. As the paper suggested, he is the individual who gave Dr. Westbrook the $2,000,000."

"Not too bad," Vlassak says, looking at me again. "Perhaps I should write a large volume dealing with the Germans of the Sudetenland." He continues. "Now the four of us are to meet at one-thirty for lunch at the Prague Cafe with Mr. Emil Naumann, an important member of the Czech legislature."

"Name sounds German," I tell him.

"Naumann is, of course, a German name, but I can assure you, he is a Czech citizen. I should warn you, Dr. Westbrook, he is perhaps the one person who may possibly be able to persuade you not to publish your manuscript."

"I'm looking forward to meeting him, even though we may disagree." Before we leave his office Vlassak hands me the section of the Prague paper that contains my article. He then gives us precise directions to the Prague Cafe, actually not too far away. We agree to meet there at one-thirty.

I return to my hotel and knock on Everly's door. She is not there. I can only assume she has finished reading my many e-mails and has now either taken a walk in the city center, or has perhaps gone over to the 'Little Section' to visit Wallenstein's palace. As for myself, I'm feeling the need for some additional rest, no doubt due to having had to practically carry Everly back to her room last night. I return to my own room, leave a wake-up call for one o'clock, and immediately fall asleep on my bed.

The Prague Cafe turns out to be an upscale restaurant. Arriving there, I meet Erik, Jonathan, and Professor Vlassak just inside the main door. We soon find Mr. Emil Naumann seated in front of a large window which offers an exceptional view of the Moldau River and the castle, much like the view Everly and I enjoyed yesterday at noon from our outdoor cafe.

When Naumann stands to greet the four of us, I find his physique leans somewhat toward shortness and roundness. I think he is probably not more than five-feet six inches tall. He is, however, one of the friendliest men I have ever met, and when Vlassak steps closer, they hug each other in hearty fashion as though they are extremely close friends. After the five of us have completed the introductions, and are seated, Naumann shares something with me which he obviously considers important.

"Dr. Westbrook, early this morning I received a call in the Czech language from someone inquiring about you. I had not yet looked at my morning Prague newspaper, and so I had no reason not to speak with the gentleman. At first his voice was pleasant, and so I mentioned I would be meeting you here at this cafe between one-thirty and three o'clock. I suggested perhaps he could at least drop by, introduce himself, and shake hands. But then, the quality of his voice changed. It became harsh, even threatening. He said: 'tell that Nazi professor he'd better never forget the Czech town of Lidice'!" Naumann is shaking his head in frustration. "Naturally, as soon as I saw this morning's paper, I knew I had made a serious mistake." He glances at Vlassak and the two Israelis, then back at me. "Do any of you believe we should change restaurants?"

"No!" I say immediately. "We remain here, as planned. If the gentleman shows up, I'll just tell him the truth, that I will never, as long as I live, forget the Czech village of Lidice."

"Good enough," Naumann replies, and then, after a few seconds, he brings us up-to-date about some additional breaking news of the early afternoon. The infamous Sergei Petroevski it seems, has come under investigation. Police have occupied his government office, and have searched his home. He himself has not yet been taken into custody. During this announcement I have been watching the faces of Erik and Jonathan but, like myself, they seem to know nothing about this development. For me, though, the name, Michael Novotny comes to mind. I can just imagine him making numerous calls from his hospital bed, shaking up the politics in Prague. He had insisted to Everly and me during our brief visit he intends to make substantial changes, once he has enough power to do so. Because of the attack in the police station yesterday afternoon, I can even imagine Chief Krecheck being ousted, and Novotny put in charge. I'm convinced Novotny is just the man to set things straight in this city!

As soon as Naumann finished his announcement about Petroevski, he turns his attention to me again. "As I just mentioned, I've read the morning papers, Dr. Westbrook. Yesterday must have been a stressful day for you and your girlfriend. Tell me, how did the crazies here learn about your big manuscript?"

A waiter comes to our table then and interrupts us, taking our orders for drinks. I order Czech beer. I am beginning to feel a certain amount of unease here at our table. It was only yesterday Novotny freed me from the home. Am I still under the influence of those people's drugs, making careless decisions about things? In the first place, the others here believe I am the author of *The Prague Manuscript*, something which could eventually place me in grave danger. Secondly, it suddenly occurs to me, I know practically nothing about the four other individuals sitting next to me. This causes me to remember Everly's words of yesterday afternoon. 'God knows what's going to happen to you tomorrow'. Naumann, Vlassak, even the two Israelis, cannot be considered more than casual acquaintances. I have known them a scant 24 hours. When the waiter finally leaves us, I turn to Naumann once again, the man with the pure German name, but who is really Czech. I do not bother to explain that Everly is not really my girlfriend.

"As to how people here learned about me," I say, picking up the conversation again, "there are perhaps three possibilities. Five years ago I completed a small documentary film entitled *Brothers at War*, which sold well in parts of central Europe. Then, last fall I completed a dissertation dealing with the Austro-Hungarian Monarchy, which, to my knowledge, sold not one copy." I laugh a little. "Finally, several large American newspapers have printed extensive articles dealing with my recent large manuscript. It is possible, I suppose, the editors in Prague received information from people in the United States. When Ms. Everly Somerset and I left for Europe a couple of weeks ago, however, I had no idea anyone here had ever heard of us."

Naumann nods and then expands the conversation to the Czech government. He is addressing all of us now. "Whenever we are graced with visitors from other countries, I feel obliged to emphasize an important aspect regarding our government here. As you all know, in any democracy there is a left, a right, and a center. In our country there is a further complication. It is fear or suspicion of Germany. Several government officials, or representatives, have been elected or appointed purely due to their negative attitudes about our neighbor to the north and west." He turns to me again. "As Professor Vlassak here told you earlier this morning, more than a little of this negativity was present in that large article today. Frankly, I wish the newspaper had not run your photograph."

"I imagine the photograph came from a paper in Bavaria," I tell him. "People there have been interested in my research for several years."

The waiter delivered our drinks and is taking everyone's order for lunch. I have ordered a schnitzel with noodles, mainly because I have not had this German dish for quite awhile. I had no idea, of course, that even as I give the young waiter the order for my lunch, the large photograph and accompanying article would soon drastically change my life.

After the waiter left us, Naumann looks over at Erik and Jonathan. "Professor Vlassak here, called me about an hour ago to let me know the two of you would be joining us for lunch. He also gave me other news. Am I to understand you are on the trail of an old Nazi war criminal, and you think he is presently in Brno?"

"Yes, we believe so," Jonathan answers. "We are traveling there later this afternoon. God knows if we'll have any luck finding the old soldier in that eastern city." He hesitates for a second or two. "Mr. Naumann, I have long been interested in the attitudes of central Europeans toward the Third Reich and its suppression of minority rights. I try and read as much as I can, and also view any pertinent films that come my way. I apologize in advance for not remembering specific titles or characters, but a couple of films remain fixed in my mind. The first film, created sometime after the war in black and white, depicted Jews being loaded onto trucks. There were no German soldiers in sight. These were Czech soldiers in charge. They even had a strange looking Nazi flag.

"In another film, partially set in Hungary, soldiers there were attacking and killing Jews. The officer in charge spoke frankly to his men. 'Look around please. See any Germans? No, there are no Germans. We Hungarians are in charge here. This is our dirty show'! And so my question is this: What was the attitude of citizens in countries such as Poland, Hungary, and the Czech Republic, as innocent Jews were being rounded up and shipped to their deaths in the East?"

Naumann's eyes narrow slightly. "That happened a long time ago and I'm certain there was more than enough blame to go around. Some people then were gravely concerned about what was occurring, others were in favor of it, and even assisted in the criminal activity themselves. But the vast majority of people simply did not care. This was also the case in our own country after the war, when thousands of Germans and Hungarians were killed and tens of thousands of others were robbed. This is simply the truth, and modern-day Czech citizens would do well to accept it."

Professor Vlassak now joins the conversation again and gives me some harsh advice. "Dr. Westbrook, we are both historians, and though I have no business telling you what to do, it is my fervent hope your now famous manuscript ends up in our beautiful river down there." He is pointing out the window now toward the Moldau.

I smile at him. "The manuscript is not with me, Professor Vlassak." I am lying again now. "I came to Prague to finish the last of my research. However, all four of you are going to receive a bound copy of our completed work." But then I think to myself: if these men believe I am going to cancel my meeting late this afternoon with Everly and those editors at the Bohemian Central Press, they are out of their minds! This is already the 21st century. I do not need to listen to Vlassak's hyperbole!

Our food has arrived now, interrupting our discussion as the five of us are momentarily distracted. Mr. Naumann is the first to speak again. "How are you dealing with the numbers?" he asks me.

I know exactly what he means. He must almost be afraid of these numbers. "We are dealing with them province by province. So many smaller books have been written, and there are many disagreements between authors. Our volume encompasses the entire history, including the atrocities. However, we have allowed the individual reader to do the overall counting. But there were a great many atrocities; there is no sense pretending there weren't. A major question we pose is: what happened in the minds of people who allowed themselves to be able to commit these heinous acts?"

"How many innocents died?" Naumann asks. "I mean, in your opinion."

"Tens of thousands of Jewish people were shipped east during the war. As far as I know, practically none returned. During the war the Nazis oppressed the Czech people here in their own land, and many were either killed or imprisoned. And then, of course, after the war the Czechs themselves began killing and displacing Germans and Hungarians. As to total numbers we are heading toward well over 150,000 people. Many more Germans and Jews, of course. Our book is disquieting, I admit it. But what would you have me do?"

There is total silence here at the table. No one takes another bite of food. Erik and Jonathan are staring at me. Naumann seems to be looking to Professor Vlassak for some kind of strength. Finally, Vlassak turns his gaze toward me. Still more silence. He seems to be considering something.

"Most Czech people," he says, "live on the bright side. In your case, though, there might be danger. And could you have read this morning's newspaper article in Czech, I actually believe you might cease your work on *The Prague Manuscript* and take up another project. A less dangerous project." I feel his eyes boring into me.

"For there is a dark side here as well, Dr. Westbrook. In this land, I mean. A dark side, emphasized by a far-off scream of agony. This scream began some distance from here on the 8th of November, 1620, when General Tilly's imperial army broke through the center of the Bohemian lines at White Mountain; it continued until the end of the First World War, and it began again when Hitler's panzers moved upon us in 1939. It is a scream that is accompanied by indiscriminate killing, and I can already sense it now, vibrating and pulsing throughout the Czech Lands. It causes me to fear you, Dr. Westbrook, and to fear for you, and it is the main reason I think you should shortly plan to leave our beautiful land."

I give Vlassak a gentle smile. I look pleasantly at Naumann, too, as well as Erik and Jonathan. I have been affected by this speech much more than I am showing. Still, I don't really believe Professor Vlassak wants me to stand and leave my schnitzel dinner while I am still hungry. I nod toward the four men once again; then, I wave to our waiter and order another Czech beer. I have not changed my mind. I still plan to keep my meeting time with Everly and the publishers later today.

The meal continues. There appear to be no additional controversial speeches on tap. Rather than further discussing my large manuscript, we return to the subject of the investigation of Petroevski, and perhaps later, Drtina. I had never heard of these two politicians before, but I understand from our following conversation, they are both Czech nationalists who distrust Germany, despise NATO, and would love for the Czech Republic to leave the European Union. The two are evidently in trouble now because of cutting corners financially, and making outlandish comments in the press. It all rather reminds me of what happened to Senator Joseph McCarthy back in the U.S. in the 1950s, though this may turn out to be even worse. While I actually find the topic interesting, I doubt it will stick in my mind much after leaving central Europe.

Later, as we are about ready to leave the restaurant, Naumann asks the Israelis at which hotel they are staying. When he discovers they are in my own hotel, just two floors higher up, he suggests it might be better for the three of us to walk along together. When Erik asks him why this should be necessary, Naumann says, while he was walking here to the restaurant, he had noticed people milling around in the city center in unruly fashion. He thinks perhaps three are better than one. I am also puzzled by this strange statement, but I have nothing against walking with Erik and Jonathan.

I have already received everyone's address in order to send them copies of our book. After giving Vlassak several of Everly's crowns to cover the cost of my meal, I shake hands with both himself and Naumann, and the two Israelis and I leave the Prague Cafe and head in the direction of our hotel. After briefly discussing the saga of Petroevski and Drtina, we return to the subject of Wilhelm Gertner, supposed Nazi war criminal. I ask again what evidence the two might have against the old German soldier, but they seem to have nothing further to add.

I don't attempt additional conversation for the moment as it is now mid afternoon, and the entire area is filled with hundreds of people. Their loud voices make any further discussion impossible. We are almost to the famous Hus monument now. Erik and Jonathan are walking on my left. Far up ahead I see a small crowd gathering. It seems a scuffle has broken out. But then I notice something totally unbelievable occurring on our right. In seeming slow motion I see Hus's communion cup, along with his hands and wrists, fly fifteen feet into the air and float somewhere off to my right and drop to the ground. Weirdly enough, at first I sense no danger, because I hear no sound. But then I see both Erik and Jonathan fall on my left, and I know we are facing a long-range sniper, probably situated in a window high up in some distant building. He had been zeroing in his sights when he hit the Hus monument. I dive forward toward the monument and a little to the right, and then roll. They may have torched the old warrior preacher in Constance, but by God, the remainder of his statue still has a lot of heft and weight! I lie behind it in relative safety, waiting for help to arrive.

I already know my left chest and upper left thigh have been hit. I have touched these areas and noticed blood on my right hand afterwards. I wonder if a bullet has also struck my left lung. I can't tell. If so, blood will soon be coming from my mouth. This is unbelievable! It turns out I was safer in the home!

Although there had been only enough time for a fleeting glance, I some-how feel Erik and Jonathan are dead, either from shots to the head or neck. The shots had come from their direction, and their bodies had at first protected me somewhat from the gunman. Many of the people around the statue are screaming now, especially women and children.

I soon hear an ambulance again—that same old heehaw sound I heard yesterday and have heard so often when in Europe. Though it seems an eter-nity until they arrive, it is probably less than ten minutes. Next comes the ride in the wagon, with two Czech male nurses attempting to keep me stable en route to the hospital. I later learn that once there, the doctors operated immediately to remove bullets from my left chest and upper left thigh. I remain unconscious. Sometime in the afternoon I awake momentarily in a kind of stupor and think I see Ruth standing at the window, looking down at the streets of Prague. Do I hear her voice?

"I will stay with you until Everly arrives," she says, mentioning a young woman she has not yet met in person. Just before losing consciousness again, I think back to the frightening phone call Naumann received. Why would anyone have called him, and how would the person have known about any connection he had with an American professor? I pass out.

Sometime later my eyes focus on the hallway, my door now open for some reason, where I see a Czech policeman already on duty, guarding my room.

He is no doubt trying to protect me from the 'dark side'. I imagine Ruth is in a chair by my bed, holding my right hand. I think she gives me a squeeze, just as a nurse enters the room to take my temperature. The nurse takes no notice of my beautiful visitor. Although I am barely lucid, I remember vaguely I am supposed to meet Everly later in the afternoon. Everly does not yet know I've been shot. I need help!

"English?" I ask the nurse as she is about to leave me. "German?" She shakes her head and walks away.

The nurse left the door to my room open, which still seems a bit strange to me. But then I think they are perhaps relying on the young policeman to glance in on me once in awhile. In my drugged-up state I think back to 1939 and that big Mercedes, moving slowly along in Prague. The German driver, attempting to steer a steady course through the streets, the tall Czech policeman along side, holding back the mostly angry crowd, protecting the Chancellor sitting in the back of the Mercedes, even though most Czechs would consider him the enemy. For the policeman guarding me there in the hallway now, many would say our manuscript is actually his enemy. Yet there he stands, faithfully guarding me. I take a small breath.

I simply must find someone to make a couple of calls. I have to reach Everly, either at our hotel, or the Bohemian Central Press. It is only much later I learn the editors at the publishing company have canceled our appointment for the afternoon, due to massive negative press coverage about our manuscript, and the attacks that occurred yesterday. It appears I am helpless. I lose consciousness again.

I do not know how long I slept. Looking out into the hallway, I now see there are two guards stationed there. A few minutes later a third guard arrives to join them. The third guard is an American marine from the embassy here. Two Czech policemen, plus the marine. Surely, that ought to do it!

It can't have been much later that my surgeon, whose name I learn is Kazak, enters my room, followed by Professor Vlassak and Mr. Naumann. Kazak knows my left chest is injured and so he merely raises his hand in greeting. He tells me he wishes to give me an update concerning my condition. Meanwhile, I have nodded to Vlassak and Naumann, my face expressing surprise they have heard of the attack on me so quickly.

"The bullet luckily missed the lung by half an inch," Dr. Kazak tells me. "Of course, you're obviously aware of your injured upper left thigh, though this is not nearly as serious. The good news?" He is smiling now. "I am fairly certain you will live. I should like to keep you here a few days, but I must warn you, certain powerful people in this city would prefer you leave the Czech Republic within hours. I intend to fight them on this." Kazak turns to Vlassak and Naumann now. "These two gentlemen have asked to visit for a few minutes. They are concerned you might need to phone someone, or perhaps send an e-mail or letter. They will only be allowed ten minutes; then I want you to rest again. There are a lot of drugs in your system. You won't have any trouble sleeping. I will naturally be back in a couple of hours." He nods again and leaves us.

"I deeply appreciate this," I tell Vlassak and Naumann. "I really do need a bit of help. I somehow need to reach Ms. Everly Somerset by phone. She will either be in her hotel room, or at a publishing house called the Bohemian Central Press. She needs to learn I have been shot."

Within a couple of minutes Naumann, having taken the phone book from a drawer in my small bedside table, has called both numbers. Everly appears not to be in her hotel room, and people at the Bohemian Central Press informed Naumann she had left that establishment a long time ago, actually shortly after four o'clock. Naumann had left a message for Everly at the hotel. I was smiling as the diminutive Naumann wrestled with the big phone book. Of course, I could not have managed this at all in my present condition.

I have already noticed both men appear deadly serious. They do not bother hiding the news. Erik and Jonathan, the two Israelis, are dead. Neither man had even lived to make it to the hospital. This is about what I have suspected myself. I had vaguely heard a second ambulance coming as I was being carted away. I actually feel beholden to the Israelis, for they had shielded me from the first of the firing. It is difficult for me to believe they are gone. Although we had met only yesterday, they seemed to be honest, hardworking individuals. I am always amazed at how quickly a couple of human lives can be snuffed out.

Vlassak and Naumann do not stay long. They have not forgotten Dr. Kazak's advice. Naumann brings me up-to-date on what has been happening during the past hours. Two additional articles have appeared in other smaller newspapers, both with photographs. The one photograph is from five years ago, and shows me filming in the Sudetenland with a large video camera. The radio and television stations are evidently also hard at it, dealing with my case several hours a day. Naumann tells me I am being referred to by some as that 'Nazi Professor from Denver, Colorado'!

Vlassak walks to the television set, situated high up in my room. He flips through three channels, one after another. I am astonished to find the commentators all discussing *The Prague Manuscript*. This is obvious to me because the words are interspersed with various scenes from the city center. I see flashes of unruly people in the streets. Again, I see a couple of clenched fists, as had been so evident there in 1939. Two men in a crowd have begun shoving each other, perhaps a democrat against a nationalist, perhaps a person on the 'bright side' versus another on the 'dark side'. "I just can't believe this is happening," I tell my two guests. "And to think, the two Israelis died because of my manuscript. I find it incredible this subject still provokes so much disorder here. It all happened so long ago."

"I suppose it is rather like your own civil war," Naumann says. "Certain people will never be able to forget it."

"We have little time," Vlassak says, glancing at his watch. "There are a couple of other matters to discuss. First of all, there is no word of the sniper being apprehended. Disappeared into thin air, just like the shooters in the gray Audi yesterday. Also, there is worldwide coverage of the situation here. Your large book, Dr. Westbrook, has become famous, even before it is born."

Naumann enters the conversation again. "For this reason, the two of us would like to give you some advice. We have no idea about the situation at your university, but we wonder if you might not like to consider a year's sabbatical, until this cycle of revenge subsides. For even now you are not safe. There are three guards in that hall out there. Yet one 'crazy' with a hand grenade could wipe them out in five seconds, and then kill you after the three of them are dead."

"Well, I could probably take a year's leave of absence. And I agree this might be a good time to do it. With the donation I received from the old German soldier, I could certainly afford it. Meanwhile, according to Erik and Jonathan, this same gentleman is now under suspicion of being a war criminal, and is presently roaming around somewhere near the city of Brno. Considering my condition, I can't do anything about this, but Michael Novotny, an excellent police officer here in Prague, knows all about the old German. I think I'll let him worry about it. Maybe he can get some help out of Vienna."

I feel wiped out again, and Naumann and Vlassak are immediately aware of it. At first I think they are about to stand, preparing to leave, but then Vlassak quietly brings up one last subject. "We're wondering if you haven't been asking yourself about the phone call Mr. Naumann received this morning. As you know, we were concerned about this even before you joined us for lunch. We believe the phone call was connected to a problem we have had for several weeks, namely that one or more people have been hacking into our computers. It is even possible the person who made the threatening call knew about our luncheon meeting even before you did. You see, my friend here is the equivalent of your majority leader in the United States Senate. He is under pressure from all sides. Actually, both of us have enemies."

I meet Vlassak's eyes. "Yes, I did briefly think about the phone call, but frankly, because of what happened to me, the question slipped my mind. But how was it you learned of the sniper attack so quickly? The two Israelis and I were shot less than fifteen minutes after leaving the Prague Cafe."

At that moment I am taken aback as Naumann continues the conversation in German. Although I understand every word, I am immediately aware his German is better than my own. He explains he and Professor Vlassak had actually followed Erik, Jonathan, and myself from some several hundred yards behind, still concerned about possible unrest in the city center. Although they had not actually witnessed the attack, they were aware that something was happening far ahead near the Hus monument.

"As for my German," Naumann continues in English, "as the principal leader in our legislature, it is imperative I speak and understand German.

Germany is without doubt our most important neighbor. I know you are aware of this." Both men stand now, ready to say goodbye.

"Gentlemen," I say with emotion, "you just can't imagine how much your visit has meant to me. I am hoping the three of us can keep in touch in the future. I have appreciated your advice." Because they cannot shake hands without walking around my bed, they wave goodbye and slowly exit my room. After the two had gone, I turn and look on my right to the chair located between my bed and the window. Naturally, it is empty.

Did I fall asleep again? If I did, I could not have gotten much rest. Another visitor is standing at my door. The American marine stands ahead of him, slightly to his right. The new visitor is tall and thin and seems impatient. At first I wonder how this visitor gained access to my room, but then the marine informs me he is Mr. Avery Cranshaw, Ambassador to the Czech Republic. Naturally the marine knows him since he works for the man. The marine leaves the room after giving me a nod. I point to my chest, letting Cranshaw know I am unable to offer my left hand. He takes a seat in one of the two chairs available and immediately asks me if I have any further news about the sniper.

"Not a thing," I tell him. "I imagine you are already aware I was attacked twice yesterday."

He nods. "The news has reached the United States. This morning I received an urgent call from a senator from Colorado, raising hell about the whereabouts of his daughter. Do you also know perhaps there are presently mini demonstrations going on in the center of Prague? And just where is Ms. Everly Somerset?"

"I was supposed to meet Ms. Somerset at four o'clock this afternoon, but could not manage it due to the superior aim of our sniper. I'm not certain where she is right now. We called her hotel room less than an hour ago but there was no answer. We naturally left a message, informing her about my condition, and providing my phone number here in the hospital. I also know about the minor unrest in Prague as someone turned on my television set earlier. I find it astonishing."

"What is this regarding some manuscript? I know nothing about it."

I hesitate, though only for a couple of seconds, as I prepare to lie again. "It's title is, *The Prague Manuscript.* I have been working on it for nearly five years. It deals with the deaths of well over 150,000 innocent civilians, practically all killed during the Second World War, or within several months after that war ended. Most of the victims were Jews, Germans, or Hungarians, though many Czechs were killed during the Nazi occupation as well. There are several theories concerning the number of deaths at that time. The difference is, I know where many of the atrocities occurred, and even when some occurred."

"And perhaps because of this knowledge, the streets of Prague are becoming somewhat unsafe. There seems to be no end to these silly protests. Of course, people are protesting because you remain in their country. I imagine you know this." He hesitates, watching me carefully. "Now, due to the turmoil, I believe I have a right to examine your manuscript. Just how long is it?"

"Well over 700 pages. I'll get you a copy in the Czech language."

"I don't speak Czech. Give me a copy in English."

"I promise I will send you one from Colorado as soon as I am home. There are no copies of the manuscript here in the Czech Republic presently." I am lying again. "Now you do know, Ambassador Cranshaw, that in one of the attacks yesterday several shots were actually fired at Ms. Somerset and myself inside the main police station? At least, I assume you have heard about this."

"Of course, though problems existing in the Prague police department are actually beyond my bailiwick. I do know there has been a shakeup."

"I'm hoping Michael Novotny is now in charge."

"I'm not certain, but I believe he may be." The Ambassador hesitates for a second or two. "My people in the Embassy are handing me stories about some old Nazi war criminal, who is supposedly wandering around the Czech Republic. Know anything about it?"

"Some. My two Israeli friends told me they believe he is a war criminal and is presently somewhere in the Brno area."

"Well, this is now my affair!" I need to speak with these Israelis as soon as possible!"

"This could be problematical. You see, they are both dead."

"What! Don't tell me they were the ones killed a few hours ago when you were shot!"

"I'm afraid so. They were walking on my left. In effect, they probably saved my life. But I can give you other information about Mr. Gertner, or should I say, Officer Gertner? I met him a few weeks ago in his mansion in Lake Forest, Illinois. He gave me a donation of nearly $2,000,000 to help with the publication and promotion of my manuscript. By the way, he did not seem like a war criminal to me. He seemed like a German soldier, who had fought hard for his country."

"Is it possible this man is not even alive?"

"Possible. The men of the Wehrmacht are all dying out. But I must tell you, the two Israelis insisted he took a plane to Prague just recently. Of course, I have no proof of this myself."

"Dr. Westbrook, I need to get back to the Embassy and start working on this war criminal case." He stands and turns toward the door. "Please locate Ms. Everly Somerset as soon as possible. Call us if you need assistance." He waves farewell over his shoulder.

I have passed out again, not surprising considering the amount of drugs they must have shot into me. I awake later to find Everly in the single chair on the right of my bed, exactly where I imagined Ruth was sitting sometime earlier. She waits until she is certain I am lucid.

"We're leaving here tonight, Bob. I've ordered a private jet. Dr. Kazak and I had a spirited discussion about this, but he eventually had to agree to my plan after I promised to pay for a specialist to accompany us to Munich.

The jet will then return to Prague with the specialist on board."

At that moment Dr. Kazak entered my room. He nods to Everly, whom he has obviously already met. I notice he is no longer smiling. "I have a profound disagreement with Ms. Somerset here," he begins, looking in my direction. "You have no business leaving this hospital tonight."

I quickly glance at Everly. "I thought you said there was an agreement."

She looks coolly at Dr. Kazak. "The terrorists have fired at least 40 rounds at Bob during the past 24 hours. This afternoon they almost got lucky."

Kazak is shaking his head in anger. "You are placing this man in grave danger. Five minutes ago I called the office of the American Ambassador, requesting that people there intervene in order to keep Dr. Westbrook from leaving."

"Bet they weren't cooperative," I say. "When I spoke with the Ambassador earlier, I had the distinct impression he wanted me out of the country." I meet the doctor's eyes. "I want to thank you now, Dr. Kazak. I may not get another chance. In my opinion, I could not have been in better hands. I imagine Ms. Somerset here has already booked me into a good hospital in Munich."

"I have. And don't worry, Dr. Kazak, Bob is young and tough. He'll make it. But I do want to thank you as well. You probably saved his life."

Kazak continues shaking his head in disgust. He pats me lightly on my left wrist and only nods at Everly. I watch as he turns and vacates the room.

"I have seen some of the television coverage, Bob. You've become rather famous in a dangerous sort of way. People downstairs in the lobby all have their eyes on the big TV set. Many seem fascinated by the reports. The hospital, though, is not mentioning you are a patient here. Too dangerous." After a few seconds she brings me up-to-date concerning the Bohemian Central Press. "They turned us down, Bob. Too much controversy. They are returning the money. But don't worry. We'll have more success in Bavaria."

That I can imagine, I'm thinking.

"Now, Bob, a nurse will accompany us to the airport. The specialist will meet us there. You should know they've loaded you up with more drugs. They don't want you experiencing any pain during the short flight. In spite of his argument here a few minutes ago, Dr. Kazak has known for at least an hour that we are going to Munich. No one can stop us!"

"More drugs?" I smile weakly. "I think I can already feel them kicking in. I'm very tired."

"Go to sleep, Bob. I'm in charge of everything now." I watch as her beautiful face seems to drift toward me, and then away again. I soon pass out. I didn't have much choice in the matter.

When I awake many hours later, I see Ruth and Everly standing in the middle of my Munich hospital room hugging each other. Then they are kissing each other. Now they are hugging again. "Well," I say softly, "I'm certainly glad you girls are getting along so well." I'm still groggy. Can I perhaps have imagined this scene? I believe I see both women walking toward my bed. Then they are here, standing beside me. I seem to recall they both gently touched my face. I don't remember anything else.

Meanwhile, the world continued spinning along without me. I later learned that Everly called Ruth in Berlin, informing her of my condition. Ruth immediately altered her schedule and took a fast train to Munich. She met Everly in the hospital. Everly eventually stayed with Ruth at her large apartment, though both women remained in the hospital until well after two in the morning. I am astonished I seem to be blessed with two lovely guardian angels who are willing to spend such a large amount of time and energy looking after me. Sometimes I wonder if I'm worth it. They are keeping me here in this hospital three additional days, just as Dr. Kazak suggested. Although I did not know it until a couple of days later, it turns out Kazak has been keeping tabs on me ever since I left Prague. My new doctor is named Wilder, who visits me once a day, smiles continuously, and gives me the impression he is confident I will soon be on my feet again. He knows Dr. Kazak, and has told me my Czech physician did an outstanding job caring for me.

Thus far, the most affection I have received are a few soft kisses and gentle pats on the head or right arm. Ruth and Everly visit me a couple of times a day, sometimes individually, and sometimes together. They never stay long. Doctor's orders, of course.

Soon after arriving in Munich, I gave Ruth a complete report about my dangerous adventures in Prague, including how I was saved at one point by an honest police officer named Michael Novotny. Ruth can only shake her head in astonishment at this entire account.

It was late Monday morning that the two women visited me for the last time together, just before Ruth left for Berlin. We discussed the near future and it is then I realized that Everly and I are to be left alone in Munich. This means, of course, I will need to keep an eye on her, according to suggestions made by my university back in Colorado, and her father, the senator. I plan to alter this arrangement as soon as I can, perhaps by placing my graduate student on a plane heading back toward Denver. After a few minutes, Everly tells us she is going down to the cafeteria for coffee. I am certain she just wants to give Ruth and me some privacy.

"Hasn't been much of a reunion, has it?" I say. Instead of answering, Ruth gives me a long kiss on the mouth. She's aware I'm feeling much better now.

"It's been just as tough on me," she says finally. "Now, just as we said a couple of minutes ago, you'll be staying at my apartment for the duration, while Everly will have a room in the Bayrischer Hof." She laughs. "Can you imagine the mixed emotions I am feeling? That girl is falling in love with you, Bob. Can't you persuade her to go back to the States for a few weeks and then, if necessary, return to Europe with someone else, perhaps her father?"

"She can't stand her father. But let's consider this situation carefully. In my opinion, Everly has serious emotional problems which have led to her outlandish plans of protest against the people of the Czech Republic. They're letting me out of here tomorrow. That's Tuesday. If I haven't brought her to her senses regarding her future plans by Thursday afternoon, I'm calling her father and advising him to get over here and rescue his daughter. Then I'm heading north and joining you in Berlin."

"What about the university? Won't you need to call them, too?"

"I don't think so. Contracts are made to be broken. I'm not even certain I'm going to collect the ten grand they owe me for making this trip. I don't want them to have the slightest thing to hold over me."

"Day before yesterday Everly told me if anything ever happened to her, you'd be hearing from more than one person. Have you any idea what she meant?"

"Sure. Dr. Harald Haverkamp, President of the University, Dr. Melvin O'Roark, Vice President, and naturally her father, the senator. I really can't think of anyone else. Her poor mother in Denver is seldom lucid. A tragedy, of course, and I can't help feeling sorry for Everly for what she is facing there. I sure hope her father starts giving her additional support."

"I really like Everly. She's been consistently friendly to me, and she's so beautiful I sometimes find myself staring at her." Ruth laughs.

"She's gorgeous, all right, but she's someone who can't decide whether she's a young woman, or a teenage kid. You've surely noticed that occasionally her choice of words seem, well, adolescent, especially after consuming a couple of drinks. You know, last Friday, the day I was shot, she was supposed to be on her own right after our meeting with the editors at the Bohemian Central Press. This was our agreement. But, of course, after I was shot, there was nothing she could do except stick by me. And you probably realize that, except for Novotny and people at the police station, no one knows who she is.

No one in Europe has ever seen her photograph. It is me, the 'Nazi professor from Colorado' who some would like to kill. Not Everly. She can wander around free as a bird without fear."

"Of course, ultimately you will have to face the fact she is an adult. How long will it take to publish the various versions of the manuscript, in English, German, French, and Czech?"

"Not as long as you might think. Two or three weeks perhaps. Everything is ready to go! And I have no doubt Everly will find a publisher here in Munich. Hell, tens of thousands of people in Bavaria still consider the Czech Republic an eastern province of Germany."

"I would continue to hammer her right up to the time she drops the leaflets. After that, if she still insists on hiring all those protesters, I would not only go to her powerful father, I would go to both German and Czech officials and schedule meetings. Hiring all those destructive people to go into Prague and other Czech cities could be considered an act of terrorism! Our beautiful young genius may be getting ready to commit a serious criminal act. Considering her high intelligence, I am amazed she hasn't already thought of this. Of course, you should warn her about your plan of action in advance."

"You referred to Everly's mind. Well, in terms of research and her writing in general, she's impressed me more than any student I ever had." I hesitate for a few seconds. "But something about the present situation bothers me, and I'm not just talking about her disruptive plans. It's something else, though I can't grasp what it is. You know, I simply must get her back to the United States." I say this just as Everly joins us again. She eyes both of us. I'm quite certain she realizes we have been discussing her infamous plans for the future.

"You both surely realize I have a perfect right to spend my own money as I see fit."

"Up to a point," Ruth says. "I would draw the line at hiring the protesters."

I look up at Everly. "I agree with Ruth, and I plan to do everything I can to persuade you to drop that idea. Good God, Everly, you might be arrested!"

"That's all right, I'll take my chances." She continues looking directly at me. "I have just spoken by phone with an editor at a Bavarian publishing company. We are scheduled to meet with him at four o'clock tomorrow afternoon. I certainly hope you are still willing to be a part of this."

I nod immediately. "Of course, I'll go with you. I'll even stick with you on the idea of the full-page ads, and the leaflets, though I think the leaflets are overkill. After that, though, I won't be on board. Not regarding the protesters."

"Well, at least you're honest about it But when did you become such a coward? You certainly had the guts to strip that old German soldier in Lake Forest of half his loot, and you lied your head off to get it! But it all worked out, didn't it? Nearly $2,000,000 in that safe deposit box on County Line Road in Denver. And you have the nerve to talk about me heading to the clink!"

For a moment I do not answer her. Something is still bothering me. 'Of half his loot', and 'lied your head off', and 'heading to the clink'. I have never seen such slang phrases in our large book. But I say: "You are correct, of course, and I've always thought we should utilize some of the money in Denver to publicize and promote *The Prague Manuscript*. We'll need to discuss this aspect in detail as soon as I'm up and around again."

"Meanwhile, I'm 'detailed' out," Ruth says abruptly. "I need to catch a train." She glances at her watch. "Taxi will be waiting." She leans down and gives me another long kiss; then she stands and gives Everly both a hug and a kiss. "I hope we can keep in touch," she tells Everly. Everly nods, a bit sadly, I think.

"I rented another Mercedes, just as you suggested," Everly tells me after Ruth has gone. "I'll be here at ten o'clock tomorrow morning to pick you up." She sits down on a chair nearest my bed. "It seems a little sad that Ruth had to leave. I'm going to miss her. I hope, though, you'll be somewhat less lonely because I'm here with you."

Although I'm missing Ruth already, I still manage to give Everly a small smile. "Of course, you're a great help. But no matter what happens, there is no reason why the three of us can't remain friends in the future. We certainly have enough money to live our lives as we please."

"Up to a point. I've often heard two women can never remain friends in the long run, especially when they're fighting over the same man."

"No one is fighting, Everly."

"The hell we're not! You just haven't realized it yet. And I intend to fight like a sex-starved demon! If Ruth knew about my true feelings, she would stick a knife in my throat."

I'm laughing openly now. I just can't help it.

"Why are you laughing?"

"Because, sweetheart, sometimes you act younger than your actual age. And Ruth is not going to stick a knife in your throat." I laugh again.

"Well, damn it to hell, what really is coming next in our lives? I'll bet you're going to marry Ruth."

"I'm actually not certain about that. You see, I haven't yet asked Ruth to marry me. I thought I should wait until I am on my feet again. But speaking about the two of us, Everly, we have both been under a great deal of stress and often, at times like this, one's emotions lurch out of control. I urge you to relax and take everything one day at a time. Our manuscript will not be ready to go for at least two weeks. We don't need to make any major decisions right now. But, meanwhile, don't completely trust your feelings. Because of what happened to us, we naturally feel the need to lean on each other, almost as though we're the only people who understand. Later, it's likely you'll feel differently about our relationship. Don't you think so?"

"No, I don't. I will never feel differently! And there must be a way. I know there is! We'll just have work it out. And Ruth will help us. She cares about me."

I smile, thinking this conversation is lurching decidedly toward the childish. "I thought Ruth was getting ready to attack you," I say, acting like a teenager myself.

"Please, don't tease me. I'm deadly serious here."

I grin at her. "Well, there might be a way to work it out, though we would need the help of a time machine. The three of us could live in the mountains of Utah in the 19th century, smooch each other half to death, and have fourteen children. I say this, even though such thoughts must mean I'm living with a sizable chink in my moral armor."

"Forget about your moral armor. Let's live a little!"

"You mean, move to Utah? I believe there are laws now, even there."

"No! No! We could live in Munich, in Paris, even Denver. We could pretend I'm a younger cousin or something. We could be deliriously happy together. Hell, I'm so enamored of Ruth I'm about ready to take on the life style of that girl who lived on the island of Lesbos."

"You mean Sappho, the ancient Greek poet?"

"Yes. I can envision Ruth and me devouring Sappho's 'pure love lyrics' together. You could even join us."

"Well, that sure sounds like a plan. Perhaps we could enjoy her poetry in the original Greek." I laugh.

"That might be carrying things a bit far," she says absently.

I look at her seriously now. "Everly, I have a question. How much alcohol have you been consuming recently? I'm guessing quite a bit."

"Some. It helps me sleep. Why should you care? I'm 22. Surely, I can drink as much as I like."

"I suppose so. It also seems you've been overly nervous of late." I hesitate. "Of course, considering what has happened, it's a wonder we're both not nervous wrecks. Look, why don't we finish our work here as soon as possible and then return to the United States. Relax a little."

"What about Ruth?"

"I'm quite certain Ruth will be visiting us in Colorado sometime in June. The three of us can get together then."

"Ruth could stay with me in my mansion on Bellview."

"Sounds good. I know she would enjoy that."

"We're still facing the problem of two women and one man. It's really not fair, though I guess it's just the way things are." She grins at me. "You nice guys always get most of the goodies."

"You know, Everly, I have a feeling you are the kind of girl who starts out loving a man to distraction; then later comes to the realization the relationship is somewhat boring after all, and opts out. As I said a couple of minutes ago, you sometimes appear younger than your actual age."

"Maybe we should just be honest with each other. Share our feelings."

"That's easy." I smile at her. "I've become fond of you, Everly. Frankly, I'm damned glad you're around."

"But you don't trust me completely. Even if we were a couple, you think after awhile I would just walk away."

"Perhaps. But don't worry about it. Remember, we go forward, day by day." I hesitate for a moment. "Another question for you. How did you happen to choose Professor Karl Donner to provide the basic facts for the manuscript?"

"Professor Donner was 15 years old in 1945. His childhood was spent in the Sudetenland. He witnessed so many horrific incidents there as a young man, he soon vowed to dedicate his life to researching what actually happened during those months after the war."

Everly already appears nervous. I decide to probe a bit further. "What sort of things has he published to date?"

"Oh, something called 'Benes, Evil Incarnate', 'Germans of the Sudetenland', That sort of thing."

"At his age there must be more. What else, Everly?"

"Well, he continues working on his masterpiece."

"Which is? And how long is it?"

"I'm not certain he's decided on a title yet. But I imagine it will be a very large volume."

"Describe it, 'girl child'. What's the subject?"

"Well, I really don't know. Professor Donner and I were mostly busy discussing my own manuscript." She stares down at me. "Why are you so interested?"

"Oh, just fascinated, I guess. You see, I am already of the opinion that Herr Donner completed a huge work approximately four years ago, and sold it to you for a large sum of money. For a professor, even a full professor teaching in the Chicago area, two or three hundred thousand would be a powerful incentive. I assume he promised not to talk."

"You're just guessing. But again, why do you care? And I already know you're not going to turn me in to the university." She laughs. "You like me too much. So, what's the problem?"

"Oh, maybe it's because you've talked me into signing my name on a manuscript I didn't write. And it turns out you didn't write it either. These things bother me a lot. What are you trying to pull off here, Everly?"

"Professor Donner wrote every single page from the ideas expressed in the core master, your own documentary film, *Brothers at War*. I gave him a copy five years ago. At the time he had already assembled thousands of pages of pure factual material for the final version. Don't you want to know how much I paid him?"

"Not interested. After all, there are one thousand million in every billion. I imagine you still have unlimited funds. Now here's an idea. Let's put Donner's name on the big manuscript. Let him take the credit, and all the danger as well!" I glance up at her. "How'd you pay him? Not with cash, I hope."

"No, with a certified check. I also made him sign a carefully worded contract. My law firm of Emmet, Styles, and Blakely worked the whole thing out for me." She slides forward on her chair. "Look, I'm taking off, okay? We can continue this conversation tomorrow. Hospital rooms make me nervous." She leans down and kisses me on the mouth. It's quite obvious she has no intention of discussing Professor Donner further.

Everly is waiting for me the next morning when I check out of the hospital. I'm feeling a great deal better. Except for a slight pain in my chest, and even less pain in my upper left thigh, I'm convinced I'm totally on the mend. We drive directly to Ruth's apartment where Everly waits patiently as I unlock the door.

"I'm not going to allow you to hire the protesters," I tell her while we are still standing in the middle of the living room.

"You can't stop me! I'm planning to freeze the Czech Republic for days and days! The resulting chaos will be so deadly it will be chronicled in European history texts for 100 years!"

I meet her eyes. "Everly, I'll stick with you through the leaflet business, though I feel it's redundant, but after that, I'm drawing the line. If you insist on hiring those tens of thousands of protesters, I'm turning you over to the authorities. What you are planning constitutes an act of terrorism!"

She is very quick. Her first blow bloodies my nose. The second rocks me back a step and cuts the left side of my mouth. She has struck me with such intensity the knuckles of both her hands are bleeding. I stare at her. "Want another shot? Go easy on my left chest, though. Another inch and I would have lost a lung."

She glares at me for a couple of seconds; then she collapses against me and soon we are wildly kissing each other. "For Christ's sake, take me to bed!" she mutters.

I make love to Everly for more than two hours, though it was actually more like having wild sex for two hours. During this time I was surprised to find I experienced quite a lot of pain in my chest and upper left thigh. I pressed on, though, like a soldier charging some unknown enemy position. It's the way I've always been, feeling a certain responsibility to the woman to whom I am making love. I'll probably be back in the hospital tomorrow.

Afterwards, we lie there together, not saying much of anything. I see there is some blood on our pillows, coming I'm sure from Everly's knuckles, my nose, and the left side of my mouth. Her head has been resting on my right arm. Suddenly, she pulls my arm from under her head. "Just as I expected," I say. "You're leaving me already."

"I'm going to the bathroom, Bob."

I watch her. "Well, if so, why have you staggered six feet in the wrong direction? And why are you holding onto the dresser with both hands? Might you possibly need assistance here?"

"Shut up, Bob! I'll admit some women might consider you to be too much of a good thing, but you don't need to brag about it!" The bathroom door finally closes behind her.

Later, when she returns to our bed, she closes her eyes and appears to be trying to sleep. I head toward the bathroom myself, but when I reach the door I turn back and look down at her. "I was just kidding you, Everly. I've never thought I was anything special." Later, in bed, I put my arm around her again and hold her hand. Everly Somerset has become precious to me, I think. Just like Ruth, though I sometimes wonder if I will marry either of these young women.

Our meeting with the Lindenhof Publishing Company at four-o'clock was entirely friendly and we were given a great deal of encouragement. Naturally, they could not examine 700 plus pages while we were sitting there. The two editors, Arnold Baumann and Heinrich Schultz, suggested we give them ten days and then call for another appointment. Although I have not read every word in this manuscript, I am almost certain Professor Donner's paragraphs are so superior to most things written today, the work will be accepted. The only question for myself is: in what manner do I include my name here? I have already decided I will not list myself as co-author. I didn't write any of it, unless someone counts my documentary film in the mix.

Leaving the Lindenhof Company, I ask Everly if she might not like to return to Denver for a week or so.

"What in hell is back in Denver?" she replies. "My mother won't even know I've been gone. And there is no time. I'm leaving early in the morning for the Czech Republic. I'm touring much of the country in a helicopter. It's the same firm that will be dropping the millions of leaflets later." She stops abruptly. "Say, something is wrong! I feel faint. Seems like I might have the flu."

"You're hungry," I say, laughing. "You haven't had a morsel of food since breakfast, and in the meantime you've had a lot of exercise." I smile at her.

"Treat me to dinner," she says.

"I'll go with you, but surely you'll remember I don't have the funds. I spent most of your crowns in the bar that night in Prague. We'll have to spend even more of your money here in Munich. Of course, here we'll need euros. And I insist you limit yourself to two drinks this evening. I don't want to be stuck with a drunken wench again." We are both so hungry we stop at the first decent restaurant we see.

We take our time with dinner and Everly cooperates by limiting herself to three drinks. Within 20 minutes or so she has persuaded me to accompany her on the trip tomorrow morning. I plan to buy a big cap with a bill, one I can pull down nearly over my eyes. Of course, Everly is perfectly safe. No one knows what she looks like. We hadn't even finished our salads when she asks me about my feelings.

"I hope to hell you aren't the kind of man who experiences pangs of guilt just because he makes love to a girl who really cares about him. Don't forget, I would go anywhere with you. Bucharest, Borneo. Name it!"

"Impressive, though I believe Borneo is now a part of Indonesia, and the actual land that was Borneo has a new long name beginning, I believe, with a 'K'." I grin at her. "So, I gather you are of the opinion I should feel no guilt for our escapade earlier today."

"It was a lot more than an escapade, and you know it! And besides, as far as I know, you haven't asked Ruth to marry you yet, which means the two of you aren't even engaged. And I can assure you, Ruth Wedemeyer will never go with you to Bucharest or Borneo. Hell, she won't even go with you to the United States, except perhaps for a visit. Are you really certain you want to marry this girl and spend the rest of your life in Germany?"

I hesitate. "I'm not certain about anything right now, Everly." For several seconds we are quiet as we deal with our dinner. Finally, she takes another sip from her scotch and water, and turns to a new subject.

"The day after we arrived here I was on the phone with Novotny for more than an hour. He has been made chief of police now, and he filled me in on a great many things, some of them I imagine you already know about. Two individuals named Drtina and Petroevski are presently under indictment for reasons I still don't completely understand."

"I heard about those two at lunch that day. What else did Novotny tell you?"

"I'm certain you'll remember the name, 'Kriegsbaum'. Well, the gentleman doesn't exist. The name was created by this same Drtina person. He used the name to generate tension between Czechs and the Sudeten Germans living in Bavaria. He insisted no Czech should ever trust a Bavarian. Amazing, isn't it?"

"What about Officer Gertner? Has he been apprehended?"

"Not as far as I know. My guess is, unless Israel brings additional pressure on the Czech government, nothing much will happen. Novotny explained he had already called the authorities in Bruenn, which was about the extent of what he could do." I look at her, waiting for more.

"We discussed German and Czech relations for several minutes. Naturally, he asked me again about the manuscript. I repeated what I had told him before, that he would soon be receiving his copy in the mail. Of course, I didn't share any of my future plans for his country. I didn't want to spoil his day." I see she is smiling now.

"And so, what did he say about current Czech-German relations? Are they improving? I can only think they are."

"He was quite clear about this. He said they are slowly improving, but he also insisted that, for the Czech people, Germany is still their *Schicksal*, whether they realize it or not. In other words, most Czechs remain uneasy about their powerful neighbor to the north and west."

I look at her. "You do understand the word, Everly, I mean, since you used it?"

"Of course. It literally means 'fate', or 'the force of destiny'. I prefer to think of Germany being a force of destiny for the Czechs. This is obvious when one considers the number of e-mails being sent. Novotny told me there are at least six times as many e-mails flying from Prague to Berlin, Dresden, and Munich these days, as vice versa."

"Well, that I can understand. Although the Czechs may not like it, Germany is the most powerful state in Europe, and critical to the Czech economy. But it has to be even more complicated, Everly. Feelings between Germans and Czechs have to be buried under so many layers we may never be able to comprehend them."

Everly laughs. "Well, whatever it is, you can bet your butt Eduard Benes had a hand in it."

"Of course, but could that speech he gave in Brno really have enflamed so many? And who in hell was Benes? Surely no great Czech hero. Good Lord! He spent the entire war hiding out in England!"

"Basically the Czechs were resentful because Germany had occupied their land in 1939. And then, of course, there was Lidice, a tragedy that fit perfectly into Benes' overall plan. After his paratroopers bombed Reinhard Heydrich, the man overseeing the Protectorate, the Nazis naturally killed thousands of Czechs in revenge. That's why Czech resentment turned to hate by the end of the war. After the destruction of Lidice it was easy for Benes to enflame their emotions."

I nod. "I actually think you've hit on the truth, Everly. But what happened later was totally unfair, because practically none of the 3,000,000 Germans, some whose families had lived in the Czech Lands for hundreds of years, had any prior knowledge of Lidice. Most of them had no more to do with planning the destruction of that village than some citizen of France or Italy. Tens of thousands of them were killed later because they were culturally German, which was enough for the Czechs, even though it was known at the time that few of the Sudeten Germans had much to do with Lidice."

"But for Benes, the Czech leader, who left England and returned to Prague at the end of the war, it was easy to spread hatred against the German minority. He had always planned to expel his German citizens, and now he quickly instigated his infamous decrees, which gave him the power to do it!"

"Yes, he blamed most of Czech troubles on the Germans. But this is just another example of how one jaded leader can use a particular act of revenge, namely the total destruction of the village of Lidice by the Nazis, as an excuse to terrorize another segment of his own society. One act of violence often begets another. You really ought to be considering this as you contemplate your future plan of action, Everly."

She smiles. "Don't worry. I'm contemplating everything. Do you know about the television cameras yet?" I watch her carefully, waiting for more information. "They will be situated on many of the busiest street corners in the city centers, filming exactly what is happening to my protesters."

"I think I already know what will happen," I tell her, frowning a little.

"Really. Well then, tell me."

"Okay, but first I have a question. Where are you getting these protesters? And how do you know you'll even be able to find any protesters?"

"Oh, I know. While you were being held prisoner in that home, I was busy in Slovakia among other places. I have my own Lieutenants hired; they are already firmly under my command. It's amazing what unemployed young men in the area are willing to do for a job. They are being paid $100 an hour! They have promised to give a good account of themselves." She looks at me seriously. "Now let's have your report concerning our first protest which, by the way, will be in Prague."

"I'll give you my appraisal, though I remind you that before any of this happens, I plan to have you sitting before various officials, being interrogated regarding your future disruptive plans." I take a deep breath. "Well, okay, here goes. . .

"First the police will attempt to arrest your people and take them away, but when wave after wave of additional protesters attack, tear gas will be used, in an attempt to drive them back. But there are too many. Soon the police are retreating themselves. Your protesters become emboldened and begin attacking the officers. After only ten minutes the Czech government moves intelligently, and calls out the army.

"Now your people are facing automatic weapons. Meanwhile, the red lights on the television cameras give evidence the violence is being recorded. Another wave of protesters attack from behind. They wrestle with both the police and the soldiers. Many of the newcomers are carrying long clubs or truncheons. By now several people have been injured. The police and army are losing this struggle. The Czech soldiers realize they will have to begin firing into the crowd.

"The cameras continue recording the mayhem. Thousands of onlookers hold smaller cameras and cell phones high above their heads. The scenes of violence are now being filmed from a hundred different perspectives.

"It has become a pitched battle. Most of the cameras and phones are still held on high, but some onlookers, having become fearful, have melted away from the scene." I take a quick breath. "And will the Czech soldiers really begin firing?"

"Will they?" Everly asks quietly. She is smiling serenely. "Well, at that moment, with Prague on the verge of bleeding before the whole of Europe, I will begin to believe I have won! And, with the news media in a total frenzy, growing more enflamed with every city we disrupt, it will soon be time to introduce our large, beautifully bound manuscript, which contains page after page documenting Czech crimes against German and Hungarian citizens after the big war. The western world will most certainly respond."

"And your final objective?" I ask, my eyes locked into hers. The wait seems an eternity.

"Historical truth," she answers finally, her green eyes flashing.

Later, I will think back and realize this was the last meal we would ever share. I would also remember that Joan of Arc, also a champion of her own brand of 'historical truth', was eventually burned at the stake.

Following our dinner, Everly drove me back to Ruth's apartment so I can call Ruth in Berlin and then get ready to hit the sack. Everly makes no move to come inside with me. She reminds me she'll be here at four o'clock in the morning for our trip into the Czech Republic. Before driving away to her room in the Bayrischer Hof, she hands me several thousand crowns and euros for future use. "One never knows," was her final comment.

Later, Ruth and I talk on the phone for at least 40 minutes, discussing everything from Everly, to our own future. I gather Ruth is waiting for a proposal of marriage, but I also get the impression she is still interested in having me examine the educational job market here in Germany. I tell her Everly left me an hour ago, and is presumably already in her room in the Bayrischer Hof. I do not mention Everly and I are planning to leave early in the morning for Prague. I know Ruth would vigorously oppose this trip. We agree to talk again tomorrow evening.

I slowly put on the pajamas Ruth had given me in the hospital and prepare to head to bed. While I would never have shared this information with Everly, I have to admit my session with her earlier today had practically wiped me out! I need sleep! I set one of Ruth's alarm clocks for three a.m. and crash!

Shortly after nine o'clock there is a knock at the front door and I find Everly standing there, holding a medium-sized suitcase in her right hand. "Sorry," she says, "but it was just too cold and lonely in my room in the hotel. Have you called Ruth yet?"

I give her a half smile. "I told Ruth you were long since gone. She seemed rather pleased about this."

"Life is fleeting, Bob. I need to be with you. If Ruth wants you, she'll just have to fight harder. Would you like me to call Berlin and explain the situation?"

I shake my head. "Everly, I think earlier we were a bit rough on my two injuries."

She has set her suitcase down and is standing there with her hands on her hips." Well, is your upper left thigh throbbing wildly? Has blood started running down your left arm? If not, I pronounce you fit! Just let me take care of the situation." She pushes me into the bedroom and then hops onto the bed like a 12-year-old, her head bouncing up and down on a pillow, causing the entire bed to shudder. "Come on! Come on! Let's go! Join me! I've been thinking about this for two hours!"

I'm about ready to beg for mercy. But when I slowly join her on the bed, she only laughs at me. "Scared you, didn't I?" She snuggles close and I take her hand. It is then I realize she has been drinking heavily, probably in the hotel bar. Sometime later I am vaguely aware she has put on her pajamas, though I had not even realized she had left our bed. Later still, she whispers in my ear, mostly gobbledygook, weird stuff from the Battle of White Mountain like: "Use the sword, Bob. Get the tall one! No! No! Don't just poke him. Aim for the throat! Stand aside, Bob. I'll take care of it! Now, get that snarling short guy! Can't stand snarling!"

By now I am totally awake. With my free hand I softly begin stroking her hair, hoping to calm her down. But she quickly grabs my hand again and bites it hard! It is then I realize Everly is drunk! Briefly back to White Mountain.

"Go, General Tilly! Hit the center of their line! We've got 'em now!" She gasps! "God, Bob, you're the complete man!" I take back my hand thinking: Lord, she's comparing me to Tilly! But I've had enough. I quickly turn her toward me and kiss her hard on the mouth until she finally relaxes. But now she reaches for my upper left thigh. "It's not yet throbbing," she says, laughing. "How's the chest?" I don't answer her. She pats my right shoulder. "I think my life is about to change," she tells me.

"Really?"

"Yes, I'm almost certain I'm going to marry you."

"But I haven't asked you yet." I smile at her there in the dim light.

"Don't worry, you will. You'll eventually beg me to marry you." She hesitates. "So, what's on the agenda now? You seem fit. How do you feel?"

"I feel robust," I say. "Full of pep!" My voice has taken on a contrived raspy quality. In that instant she appears to move an inch or two away from me. "Everly, you come back here! Life is short! Not to be wasted!" But she doesn't seem to listen.

"Bob! Bob! Hang on a minute here. I've had quite a few drinks, and we have a long drive tomorrow. Maybe we should just snuggle up and go to sleep. You won't be too disappointed, will you?"

I shrug. "I'll be disappointed, but I'm not going to be a bother about it." I pretend to be crestfallen. Everly is so tired she has no strength to comfort me. She is almost asleep when she whispers one last time.

"I love you, Bob. I'll never love anyone else."

"And you are an absolute sweetheart, Everly," I tell her. Thank God, I say to myself. That was a close one.

I awake sometime in the night. Everly is asleep and I am still holding her hand. I had awakened in a state of shock, suddenly realizing that one day soon I will need to turn her over to the authorities. Otherwise, she will already be in hiding, probably somewhere in Slovakia, giving her Lieutenants orders to prepare for the next large protest, perhaps in the Czech city of Brno.

I gaze at her there in the partial darkness: my revolutionary 'girl child', my beautiful seeker of truths; the eight boxes containing her manuscript, transported with us in our plane from Prague that night, safe, at least for now, in Munich. I know we should not be returning to Prague tomorrow, but if I argue with her and refuse to go, she will simply make the trip alone. I expect she'll want me to drive part way, which I'm certain will be no problem. I'm more concerned about making some stupid mistake in general due to lack of sleep.

I close my eyes and think of Ruth. I remember our first meeting outside the Nymphenburg Palace, our exciting evening in downtown Munich, and the next day's visit to Salzburg. These remembrances come to me slowly, as though in a dream. The afternoon in Garmisch, the two nights in Friedrichshafen on Lake Constance, and our night at the opera in Vienna with the snow. Such thoughts finally relax me and when Everly, always ready to help, gives my hand a gentle squeeze, I fall asleep.

In the morning I awake to find Everly dressed in male attire and wearing a New Orleans Saints cap. I tell her she is the most beautiful boy I have ever seen. Later, we cross the Danube at Regensburg, where I purchase my Bavarian-Munich soccer cap at an autobahn rest stop. We then meet the new autobahn east of Nuremberg which will take us to Prague.

After crossing the Czech border, Everly stops at the first restaurant and filling station she sees, and turns the keys over to me. I fill our Mercedes with gas while Everly goes inside to pay. Later, she comes out with two cups of coffee and a couple of kolacky. After skirting Pilsen, I press on toward Prague.

The company with the helicopter is not even a half mile from the castle and the Moldau River, and we arrive there even before the scheduled time for liftoff. Before going into the office to discuss our rental, Everly removed her Saints cap for some reason, even though I keep my soccer cap pulled far down, almost over my eyes. Everly pays half the cost of the trip then, and within ten minutes we are on our way. A second man in the office had looked up from his newspaper at Everly a few times, but this doesn't surprise me, considering how attractive she is. I've gotten used to men staring at her.

She has a special map which pinpoints places where atrocities occurred in the months after the war. I know she is also thinking about the millions of leaflets which will be dropped at a later date. Our pilot occasionally receives messages from his home base in Prague but, because he is speaking Czech, I have no idea what is being discussed. Of course, he and Everly often converse in English.

Our first fly-over is of the small city of Tabor, not a lengthy distance south of Prague. As soon as we are finally hovering over the ancient city, Everly turns back to me. "Just wanted to remind you, Jan Hus completed some of his major writings at a castle near here. Also, there is a large statue of Ziska in the city center. He was the partially blind revolutionary who reacted violently to the death of Hus. His peasant army destroyed structures throughout a wide area of central Europe."

Because I know Everly often plans to turn toward me to explain our position, I think it might have been better had she sat back here with me. Of course, she also needed to give our pilot directions. She glances at him now.

"To the southeast," she says loudly. "Nikolsburg."

"That's on the Austrian border," I say. "We're by-passing Brno, the most important city in Moravia."

"For me it will always be Bruenn! But don't worry. We'll be coming back. First, though, I want to see the big cross, and also the place where my grandmother was raped."

I notice Everly has been speaking quite loudly, and I place my right forefinger to my lips, hoping to quiet her down a little. I already know our pilot speaks and understands English, as he has been following her directions precisely.

During this rather long flight to the town of Nikolsburg, I observe the striking landscape below. Surely we are passing over Iglau, Trebitsch, and Pohrlitz, all places where atrocities occurred after the war. I see Everly is making copious notes.

When we finally approach Nikolsburg, we drop lower, almost as though we are about to land. On my right I see the large cross, which marks the end of the 'Death March', just across the Austrian border. And how many people died along this way? Does anyone know exactly? I'm certain there is a placard of some sort down there, but I've forgotten what number they give.

"My grandmother was raped right there," she tells me, pointing down. "In that village, which is practically on the border." She is shaking her head in anger. "If I could find that Czech son-of-a-bitch, I'd blow his fucking head off! Old though he might be!" She glares at the pilot. "Back to Bruenn!"

We land in Brno at the airport. It turns out Everly wants to visit the city center, mainly, I think, to look over the place. The pilot tells us in broken English he will refuel the helicopter while we are gone, just in case we need it. Everly and I walk briskly toward the terminal.

"This is a rather large city, Everly."

"So? Come on, let's grab one of those taxis." We find the driver speaks decent English. She gives him directions. When we finally arrive in the city center, she hands the man 50 euros and tells him to wait for us. He nods and says he won't move a meter. From his smile, I know he is pleased.

I am certain Everly is still obsessed with her special brand of negativity. Surely she's about to give me another local history lesson, most of which I know already. However, it turns out there are other more pressing matters.

"Hey, look, I see two rest rooms. Let's visit."

I laugh. "By gosh, that sounds like a plan! I'll meet you back here in a couple of minutes." But when Everly returns, she doesn't miss a beat with her history. I keep nodding my head in concert, receiving tidbits I had known long ago, when Everly was perhaps 15 years old. Still, I don't interrupt her.

"Those thousands of German people—women, children, and the elderly-—were assembled quite near here." She takes another deep breath. "I wonder how many Germans live here today." She looks around at the streets and buildings in this area of the city. "If there are any Germans here now, they had to have come back years later. Because practically every last German living here in the late spring of 1945 was dragged from his or her home, and forced to join thousands of other innocent civilians and become part of a hideous 'Death March' south to the Austrian border. The larger world community should never be allowed to forget this outrage!"

She is again scanning the streets and buildings, but soon spies a woman of perhaps 30 coming out of a bakery with a white sack, probably containing some bread or kolacky. Everly walks up to her and, without the slightest introduction, demands to know if she has heard of the 'Bruenn Death March'. The woman appears frightened and replies in Czech. She attempts to walk away. Everly grabs her firmly by the shoulder and demands an answer in English.

The woman stares at her. "Was not yet born. Have heard stories. Believe German people were marched south to Austria at end of war."

Everly is glaring and shaking her head. "Yes, and some thousands of them died en route! Your parents and grandparents possibly had something to do with it!" She gives the woman a hard shove.

"Good God, Everly, was that really necessary?" I see the woman hurrying away.

"Damned right!" She stomps her right foot! "Oh, to hell with this! Let's get back to the helicopter!" The taxi driver is faithfully waiting to return us to the airport.

Several miles straight north of Brno is Landskron, and Everly orders our pilot to drop our altitude, and for several seconds we hover over the cemetery and the town square. Viewing this scenery brings back strong memories to the time when I was here with my film crew, now more than five years ago.

Later, as we fly over Koeniggraetz, I remind Everly there had been a large battle here in the last half of the 19th century between Prussia and Austria, and that Bismarck and the Prussians had won. She laughs contemptuously as she glances back at me, asking if I really didn't think she knew this already.

On and on we fly, and the towns and small cities eventually become a blur, even though I'm certain I've traveled by car through many of these areas before. I look out my window toward the forested landscape. "There is a town down there somewhere called Gablonz," I say. "It has to be there."

"So? What's the importance?"

"I met an old man there once in the town center. It was when I was making my documentary film. He told me a story. He had fought at Stalingrad with the German Army, and was taken prisoner by the Soviets. It was years before he was able to struggle home. Home was Bohemia, Everly. Right here! The Czechs were able to give him only a small pension. I gave him 40 euros. I've never forgotten that man."

"I'm glad you told me about this," Everly said. I notice she is smiling.

"I glance ahead toward our pilot, trying to see if he is paying attention to our conversation. Because I cannot see the man's face, there is no way to tell. Everly continues to write steadily, and glances occasionally at her map.

I am staring out the window. "Look, there's Aussig on the Elbe!" I say. "I can see the bridge."

Everly folds away her map and booklet. "So, I'm finished." She looks at the bridge and small city. She tells the pilot to turn back toward Prague. He follows instructions.

When we land many minutes later, I leave Everly to settle our bill and walk directly back to our car. I still have the keys in my pocket. Everly joins me about ten minutes later and instructs me to drive to the castle. She tells me she has never had a chance to visit it. It is at that moment I make the most tragic mistake of my life. As I turn on the ignition I am totally relaxed because I know no one could have recognized me, not with my soccer cap pulled down nearly over my eyes and, of course, no one knows anything about Everly. I do not notice we are being followed by an old beat-up German Ford, nor do I notice when the driver of this junker passes us and drives on, while I'm preoccupied looking for a legal parking area. I must have been totally oblivious. Later I learn the man had carefully eased his car right up on the castle lawn, not giving a damn what the authorities did with it after hauling it away. Had I been aware of these things at the time, I would have yanked my cap even further down, and told Everly we would not be visiting the castle today, but would instead head back toward Nuremberg, and then on south to Munich.

But nothing registered with me at the time. Instead, Everly and I left our car after legally parking it, and strolled leisurely toward the castle hand in hand. Not far from one of the castle's main gates is a small outdoor cafe, perhaps 70 yards away. I tell Everly I have already visited the massive castle on three different occasions and I would prefer to stay right here at this cafe and order a cup of coffee. She nods in an understanding way and says: "See you, Bob. When I come back I'll have a cup of coffee, too." I smile as I watch her stroll on ahead and enter the castle. Occasionally she can be a totally nice and agreeable person.

Ten minutes pass. I am on my second cup of coffee. By now, Everly will be quite high up in the castle, probably enjoying a view of the Moldau River and the city beyond from one of the windows there. It is one of those perfect spring days. Occasionally, in the late fall, there is smog in Prague. Not today. Now, in the springtime, the air is perfectly clear and there is not a breath of wind stirring. It will still be at least 25 minutes before Everly is back. There is a tiny shop next to this cafe, and I see they are selling newspapers. Perhaps I can find a *New York Herald Tribune,* or one of the Munich papers.

It is late afternoon and there are no English or German papers still available. I absent-mindedly grab a Czech paper. I can't read it, but at least I can look at the pictures. I pay for it with some of Everly's crowns and the lady folds it in the middle and hands it to me. When I return to my table, I take another sip of coffee and open the paper. I stare at it, totally in shock! There, above the fold, are two photographs. I am on the left, Everly on the right. I am in such a frenzy to move, I tip over my chair as I begin my race toward the castle. Surely I can locate her tour group in a few minutes.

I hear the glass shatter from far above, and see a body falling, even while I am still 50 feet away. Because of the clothing, I think it is Everly. She falls silently; at least, I myself hear no sound. Women and children are screaming now, and several men in front of me are remarking about the tragedy. "Sie ist tot!" (She is dead), a German man says. "This young girl has been shot!" This coming from some American. I am unable to think clearly. I begin slowly moving to my left toward the location of my car. Thus far I have refused to look at Everly's face, though this would have been difficult anyway, because of the crowd in front of me. Still, I have to be certain. I suddenly stop and turn to the right. Using my large frame, I push forward toward her body. I take a deep breath.

It is Everly. At this point I stand there frozen, unable to move. There is more screaming now, coming from the main door. Glancing further to my right, I see two Czech policemen dragging a man outside. When they pass by me, a scant ten feet away, I realize the perpetrator is one of the two strange soldiers I had battled with more than once in the home. The police had obviously been following this man. Unfortunately, they had not arrived here in time to save Everly.

More police cars and an ambulance arrive. They will soon take her away. I walk briskly along with a crowd of other people. They all seem to want to depart the scene before being detained by the police for questioning. Emotionally I am being ripped apart! I have not yet been able to accept Everly's death. A part of me wants to learn where they have taken her, and rush there, illogical though this may be. I fight against the impulse. I tell myself my main goal must lie in escaping!

I unlock the car, stagger inside, and see my hands are shaking on the steering wheel. It is then I see the old German Ford through the rearview mirror, still parked illegally on the lawn. I become convinced the weird soldier who shot Everly carefully parked it there to be in perfect position. He then waited in the car until he was certain we were parking near the castle. At that moment he had raced ahead to be sure he could be there ahead of us.

I carefully ease out onto the street and head down the hill toward the Moldau and the main train station. Within minutes this car will be hot and so I have to ditch it. I leave it in an underground parking garage a couple of blocks from the station. I toss the keys on the floor and walk away.

I have no passport or any other kind of identification, so a train is about the only type of transportation available to me. Thank God Everly had given me those thousands of crowns and euros yesterday. Within half an hour I am on a train heading north toward Dresden. Though in a complete stupor, I cannot forget Novotny's lighthearted remark from a few days ago when Everly and I were leaving the home. It doesn't fit historically and certainly not emotionally; in fact, my own hang-up about it annoys me. Still, the phrase keeps pounding in my brain. Over and over.

'The Czechs always throw their best people out the window"!

There is no doubt a phone I could find somewhere on this train, but I have no interest in locating it. Until I cross that northern border and am safe on German soil, I have no desire to call anyone. I stare out the window at the darkening Czech countryside. I am shaking my head in despair. And so, how had it happened, this tragedy? My fractured mind returns to the beginning.

The soldier grandfather of a young American girl was shot under uncertain circumstances near Prague at the end of World War Two. Her grandmother, who had been raped during the 'Bruenn Death March' that same spring, later married into a disaster! For some years, she was forced to acquiesce to the molestation of her own daughter. The grandmother, a suicide; the molesting grandfather, fled to Central America; Everly's mother, in an institution. Had Everly been able to locate this second grandfather, I'm certain she would gladly have murdered him! It will not surprise Ruth or anyone else, that I never intend to examine this hideous family history again.

At first Everly harbored a normal kind of resentment about her past, but then, at age 18, the powerful Denver law firm of Emmet, Styles, and Blakely awarded her an extremely large inheritance, which caused her attitude to change. Now Everly had almost unlimited funds, certainly enough money to expose the postwar history of many criminal Czechs. I still do not know how much money Everly had, though she once told me the amount was in the low billions.

Although Everly and I both lived in Denver for years, we did not actually meet until she began work on her M.A. thesis at my university a few months ago. However, when she was 17, she came across a documentary film I had created, and this film stirred her in the direction of planning large demonstrations in selected cities in the Czech Lands. Since January I had attempted to guide Everly away from such plans, but obviously without success.

The last few months for me have been a combination of the weird and the tragic. Some of the occurrences, of course, happened by mere chance. In late winter, for example, I met with a retired German soldier in Lake Forest, Illinois, simply because he happened to find a large article about me in a Chicago newspaper. In his mansion, following an enlivened conversation, he presented me with almost $2,000,000 in cash to help with the publication and promotion of a large book he believed I had written. Supposedly, he himself has now returned to the Czech Republic to the Brno area.

No sooner had Everly and I arrived in Prague, than I was nabbed by a small group of ultra right-wing individuals and deposited in a home of some kind. This had nothing to do with any of Everly's plans; in fact, at the time, no one in Prague had ever heard of Everly Somerset. I was the initial focus of attention because some were convinced I had written a large volume, one with dangerous implications for the modern Czech Republic.

Even after being dismissed from the home, I was never safe. During the course of the next 24 hours, I was attacked on three occasions, and finally wounded and hospitalized. The Czech rightists were obsessed with finding and destroying *The Prague Manuscript*, and willing to go to any length to accomplish their goal.

A bizarre shock occurring in recent days was the shooting by pure happenstance of two Israeli government officials. They were sent to the Czech Republic in an attempt to locate Wilhelm Gertner, actually the same German officer who had presented me with the large donation earlier. They believed he might possibly be an old Nazi war criminal. They were also interested in our manuscript, due to its extensive coverage of Jewish history, especially during the time of the Second World War.

I will always believe Everly was affected emotionally by two circumstances. First of all, her family history, and this includes her own father, often absent from their home, and secondly, the five years she worked with Professor Donner (largely by mail) as they studied and compiled an entire history of the horrors occurring in the border areas of what is now the Czech Republic. That morning in the home, Novotny had asked me about my memory, and if I would not like to regain it. I replied: 'of course, unless all the memories from the past came together and eventually drove me insane'.

Everly had not been driven insane, though the extensive work with Dr. Donner had not left her unscathed. My own small film also had an impact on Everly, as she admitted she had watched it several times, and said it gave her a special kind of focus. She even told me on one occasion 'she could sooner blame me for her obsession, than Adolf Hitler'. That statement naturally shocked me just a bit!

Originally I believed Everly wrote the entire manuscript herself, using Professor Donner's facts, but I now know this was not true. Actually, Professor Donner (the former young man from the Sudetenland) created the large work for the most part on his own, though Everly was heavily involved with the project since she was 17. It was Everly, of course, who told me Professor Donner had carefully studied the approach I used in my documentary film, which dealt with the same subject. Everly presented him with the film five years ago, something I did not know until recently.

My problems regarding Everly began with what should have been a straightforward article printed in our university newspaper. The article was, however, later expanded and garbled by the *Denver Mountain Guardian*. By the time the story was printed in Chicago and other major American cities, Everly's name disappeared entirely, and I became the supposed author of the large manuscript. The work itself detailed the entire history of what had been Czechoslovakia, as well as injustices committed against Jews and Czechs during the Second World War, and a vast number of atrocities committed against Germans and Hungarians after that war.

I accompanied Everly to Europe, principally because I wanted to meet Ruth again and work out our future, which I was convinced at the time was uncertain. Even now I have no idea how I was identified by right-wing fanatics in Prague, but I imagine newspapers there received information about me from the American media, and then someone contacted one or more of the right-wingers. Obvious guilty individuals would include: Drtina, Petroevsky,

Police Chief Krecheck, the man and woman from the home, and their soldier type henchmen, one of whom had just murdered Everly. I also plan to talk with Novotny about the men at the helicopter company. To me, they were highly suspicious. I have also wondered why the criminals in the home didn't just kill me, as they did Everly. I can only suppose they first thought they had to find the big manuscript.

Everly was identified due to information coming from the Bohemian Central Press, the session at the police station the day before and, as recently as this morning from the man reading the newspaper at the helicopter company, when Everly and I walked in. He had most certainly recognized her from her photograph, which was directly in front of him. He had constantly been in touch with our pilot during our tour, and knew exactly when we would be returning to Prague. Because our pilot had been speaking Czech, Everly and I were unaware of what was being said. There was obviously collusion among several people, and they were able to communicate quickly. I suppose it is also possible the German publishing company from yesterday afternoon called publishing companies this morning in Prague, not to cause us trouble, but simply to learn everything they could about us.

Speeding northward, alone in my Czech train, I realize I have not yet accepted the fact that Everly is gone. I only knew her for a few months, and I'm certain I never completely understood her. Looking back, I suspect her father had shared certain information with the university administration (something psychological perhaps), and they had chosen me, as she had once said, to look after her.

And what will I remember about Everly? I can't help smiling a little now. Well, I will remember holding her hand as she slept and, of course, the two nights she was drunk! And, naturally, the one occasion we made love, just after she bloodied my face and jarred me silly! And I will remember her energy, her stubbornness, and her outlandish planning, as she prepared to pressure the present inhabitants of the Czech Republic into admitting the truth about the crimes some of their ancestors committed against their own citizens in the months after the Second World War.

She was the second girl in my story, and her young life was shattered this very afternoon in the monumental castle in Prague. And though ultimately I was unable to 'look after Everly', though God knows I tried, I now realize I had loved her, and wished I could have known her in some fashion for the rest of my life.

Dresden! The city that sustained almost as much punishment in the war as Hiroshima or Nagasaki. I have been here only once before, and at the time of that visit the large cathedral was not yet totally repaired from the fire bombing at the end of the war.

Perhaps Ruth and I might one day have a chance to come here for a visit. After going inside the station and checking the schedule for the first fast train to Berlin, I call Ruth.

This was one of the saddest conversations I have ever had in my life. As I break the news of Everly's death, my emotions scatter in all directions and I am once again overwhelmed by such grief I can hardly speak. Ruth is also shocked by the news, but she somehow remains in control, asking where I am, and when I will be arriving in Berlin. She does not waste time criticizing me for returning to the Czech Republic this morning. This is not her style. Two hours later, when I find her waiting for me in the main Berlin station, we hold each other close for a long time. When we finally walk hand in hand toward our taxi, I feel certain I will never let her go.

Postscript: Two weeks pass. Ruth and I have returned to Munich. While still in Berlin, I spoke with Michael Novotny, who saw no reason for me to return to the Czech Republic, as they had already arrested their perpetrator. He did, however, ask me about the men at the helicopter company. I said I thought they were implicated, but that I couldn't prove it. I also had a somber discussion with Everly's father, who didn't seem to blame me unduly for Everly's death, no doubt because our trip to Europe was largely his idea. When I called Harald Haverkamp, president of my university, he seemed perturbed I was not returning to my teaching position in the fall. I doubt he cares. I also spoke with my parents, who knew nothing about my recent misfortunes in Europe. And yes, before leaving Berlin, I secured a new passport.

Since returning to Munich, I have been in touch with both Professor Vlassak and Mr. Naumann by phone. From them I learned: Petroevsky and Drtina, Czech nationalists, are probably heading to prison.

The woman who held me captive in the home is still in captivity herself, awaiting trial, as are the two soldier types, the one, of course, for murdering Everly.

Mr. Krecheck, former chief of police, is under investigation. Herr Wilhelm Gertner, former officer in the German Wehrmacht, has not yet been located.

Ruth has asked me more than once about my plans for the manuscript. I have told her the large volume will be published, and small ads placed in major newspapers as funds allow. I still have the nearly $2,000,000 given me by the old German soldier. Naturally, there will be no leaflets dropped, nor any protesters hired.

It must have been in the afternoon of the third day after Ruth and I returned to Munich that a postman delivered a registered letter addressed to me from the Denver law firm of Emmet, Styles, and Blakely. I sign for it; then I walk back to Ruth and place the thick envelope in the middle of the coffee table. I gaze at it for a few seconds. Ruth and I had been sitting here drinking German white wine, and discussing our oncoming vacation trip to Colorado.

"Everly is leaving you her fortune, Bob. She hinted to me this might be the case if anything ever happened to her. Her father no doubt visited the law firm when he heard of Everly's death but, obviously, there was nothing he could do to stop the transaction. Why don't you open it?"

I meet Ruth's eyes. "Before going forward I think I should share something with you."

"Oh, I really don't think you need to," she replies.

"But I think it might be better if I explained something."

"Shut up, Bob! I have no interest in any of this. Don't you know there is not one 'real man' in the entire world who could have resisted that beautiful young girl. Hell, I could scarcely keep my eyes off her myself!" She continues looking at the envelope. Of course, she had already seen the return address. "Aren't you going to open it?"

I see her wine glass is nearly empty. I lift our bottle and refill it. I also top off my own glass. I glance down at the envelope again.

"Bob, for God's sake!"

"Just remembering something, Ruth." I smile over at her. "It takes one thousand million to make a billion." I finally reach forward and pick up the envelope.

About the Author:

Dr. James Paulding has taught more than 30 years at the university level in Illinois and Missouri, as well as directing a band for the United States Seventh Army in Europe. *The Prague Manuscript* is his seventh published book. He and his wife, Helga, have also created three documentary films, the last being *Brothers in the Storm*. They alternate between living in the Denver area and central Europe, including Germany, Austria, and the Czech Republic.